The Payroll Ambush

Whilst on its way to Fort Wilson, the stagecoach was ambushed and the army payroll stolen. Now it's down to United States Marshal Jubal Judd to investigate and bring the robbers to justice. It looks like a straight-forward assignment.

But things are not what they seem ... Why don't the robbers head for Mexico and why did they leave such an easy trail to follow?

Surely there must be someone else behind the robbery, but who could it be?

Before he can discover the truth Judd must face both danger and treachery at every step.

The Payroll Ambush

STEVEN GRAY

A Black Horse Western

ROBERT HALE · LONDON

© Steven Gray 2001
First published in Great Britain 2001

ISBN 0 7090 7011 X

Robert Hale Limited
Clerkenwell House
Clerkenwell Green
London EC1R 0HT

Typeset by
Derek Doyle & Associates, Liverpool.
Printed and bound in Great Britain by
Antony Rowe Limited, Wiltshire

ONE

'Here you are, Lieutenant.' The barkeep placed a glass of cold beer before Lucas Mariner. 'Put it on your tab?'

Mariner nodded, wondering why the man even asked. He hadn't had any money to actually pay for his drinks for quite a while and didn't now. He wondered how much he owed and was too frightened to ask; would face paying when he had to.

The barkeep wiped his forehead with the rag he'd been using to clean glasses and leaning half across the bar, said, 'Tell me, Lieutenant, is it true some Indians are causing trouble?'

Mariner nodded again. 'There are rumours of an outbreak of Apaches from their reservation down near the border. Captain Johns left with a patrol yesterday to investigate.'

Although he tried not to, he sounded dissatisfied. He would have liked to be among the men riding for the border with the possibility of being in a fight. Colonel Woodford had explained why Captain Johns

5

was the best officer to lead the patrol, the one with experience. Mariner accepted the reasons even while not liking them. He was twenty-six and needed to be given the chance to prove himself and so earn the promotion he wanted and thought he deserved. He didn't want to remain a lieutenant all his life, that wasn't the reason he'd gone to West Point and worked hard enough to graduate near the top of his class.

'D'you think the Apaches will come this far?' The bartender was worried. 'I've been involved with 'em once or twice before and I ain't got no desire to be so again.'

'I shouldn't think they would. They'd be stupid to attack somewhere so near a fort, wouldn't they? And from all I know of Apaches the one thing they're not is stupid.' Mariner spoke with authority while admitting to himself he knew little or nothing about Apaches; or any other Indian come to that. Since his arrival at Fort Wilson six months ago he hadn't even seen an Indian let alone fought one.

He downed his beer and wondered if he dare ask for another. He didn't. The Silver Spur, like everywhere else in Wilson, depended on the soldiers from the nearby fort for its livelihood but its owner was becoming irritated with having to wait so long to be paid. Anyway apart from Captain Paris, the fort's doctor, and Colonel Woodford of course, he was the post's one remaining officer. He should be there in case he was needed, unlikely though that seemed.

Leaving the town he rode the half-mile or so slowly back to the fort; it was too hot to do anything fast. As he neared the rambling adobe buildings he spotted a trooper leaning against the wall of the barracks. As the man saw him he hastily threw away the cigarette he was smoking and grabbed at the rifle by his side. Private Warren Dirkman!

'Private! Aren't you meant to be on guard duty?'

'I am on guard duty, sir.'

'It didn't look like it to me. Be thankful it's so hot or I'd put you on report.'

'Yes, sir, thank you, sir.' Dirkman gave a sketchy salute. As usual there was an insolence in his words and manner.

'And see to my horse.' Mariner dismounted and threw the reins at the young man.

Another salute, even sketchier.

Grinning, Dirkman watched as the lieutenant walked across to the tiny house he occupied on Officers' Row. Once Mariner went inside he led the horse towards the stables. As soon as he'd finished his cigarette he'd been going there anyway. Now if Sergeant Palmer saw him and asked what he was doing he had a good excuse for leaving his post.

Charley Platt and Paul Hebron, his fellow privates, were inside the dimly lit and cool stables, polishing a couple of saddles.

As Dirkman opened the door, he glanced over his shoulder to make sure no one else was in earshot and said, 'We go tonight.'

Platt and Hebron stopped what they were doing

and looked at Dirkman with a mixture of excitement and apprehension.

'You sure?' Platt asked.

He'd only just been released from the guardhouse and had no desire to be locked up again. Since joining the army he had become all too familiar with the cruel miseries thought up by cruel and miserable sergeants. He had no idea what the punishment for desertion was but beside it everything else would probably pale into insignificance.

'Yeah I'm sure. What can go wrong?'

What indeed?

'You don't wanna stay here any longer, do you?'

'No way,' Hebron admitted with a grin.

'We just don't wanna be caught.'

'No chance of that,' Dirkman spoke confidently.

Platt wasn't so sure. Any number of things could quite easily go wrong. But the reward was too great to miss out on a chance like this. To not only escape the army . . . but the rest of it as well.

Platt wasn't particularly friendly with the other two young men. He had only known them since arriving here at Fort Wilson. But they had quickly drifted together because it hadn't taken them long to realize they had a lot in common.

Which was mostly the fact that none of them was cut out for a life in the army; that the boring routine of the fort and the heat and loneliness of the desert didn't suit them. Added to which they disliked taking orders and had a knack for getting into trouble. And there were so many ways to get into trouble in the army – where punishment was swift and brutal.

Desertion was something Platt had been thinking of for a long while, almost from the day he enlisted, and the time was oh so right. While it wasn't a case of now or never, now was much better. This opportunity might not come again.

'Don't worry, Charley,' Hebron said. 'It'll be OK.'

Platt nodded, not taking much convincing.

'C'mon,' Dirkman said with a grin, 'let's go and get a nice cold beer.'

'We ain't finished polishing the saddles,' Platt objected, thinking Sergeant Palmer wouldn't like it if he knew his orders hadn't been carried out.

'Don't be such an idiot,' Dirkman jeered. 'What's the point of doing any more work when you won't be here by the time Palmer finds out you ain't done it?'

'Oh, right!' Platt stood up and stretched, hiding his annoyance. There were times when he wished he thought first before speaking and when he wished Dirkman wasn't always right. Sometimes it was good having Warren there looking out for him, other times he had a feeling the man was laughing at him.

They left the cool of the stables for the glare of the late afternoon sun. The heat was so overpowering it took their breath away as they hurried over to the sutler's store. The place was empty of other troopers and they sat at a table in the far corner.

Dirkman carried over the beers. Putting them down, he said, 'And just think we won't have to pay

for these seeing as how the payroll ain't arrived yet
and we ain't got any money.'

All three burst out laughing.

Mariner watched the three young privates crossing
the parade ground.

Trouble, he considered them.

They slouched and sauntered instead of walking
briskly. When riding they slumped in the saddle and
they handled their weapons sloppily. And despite
the efforts of Sergeant Palmer, all the time they
spent on punishment detail, they would never
change. They weren't cut out to be soldiers.

Mariner sighed. Perhaps he was being unfair. He
had chosen a career in the army, was destined to do
well. Unlike those three who would always remain
private troopers.

And while it was possible that out here in the far
reaches of Arizona there was the chance of glory in
fighting a band of renegade Apache, even Mariner
had to admit that Fort Wilson wasn't exactly the
best place to live and work. It was always hot,
always dusty and, quite honestly, monotonously
unexciting. The most exciting thing so far had been
when the vegetables he'd planted in the garden
behind his home to alleviate the fort's dread diet
had started to sprout.

Sometimes he felt dissatisfied so he could hardly
blame some of the men for their own dissatisfaction.

All the same he supposed he ought to go and find
out what Dirkman and his pals were up to. He was

certain they should be working rather than drinking. It would have been better if they had ridden out with the patrol, been given something to do.

Even as he was trying to find the enthusiasm to rouse himself, he spotted the orderly of the day leaving the post headquarters. The man was heading for his house.

And Mariner felt some relief when the man knocked, came in and said, 'Lieutenant, Colonel Woodford's compliments. He'd like to see you.'

Mariner stood up, put on his hat, and followed the orderly. Hopefully, it would be good news. The fort could certainly do with some!

Charley Platt followed Dirkman and Hebron out of the barracks. His heart was beating fast, although there was little danger of being discovered. The barracks was never more than half full and now, with most of the men away riding for the border, the room held only a scattering of troopers. They left the building to the accompaniment of undisturbed snoring.

Outside it was dark, the moon a sliver of light in the black sky. Keeping to the deep shadows they crept towards the corral at the back of the stables.

'Quick!' Dirkman whispered.

Several times, since deciding to desert, they had discussed what each was going to do. Now, as Dirkman kept watch, his two companions caught and started to saddle the nearest three horses. Platt's hands were slippery with sweat and, catching the scent of his nervousness, one of the horses whickered nervously too.

'Hush,' Dirkman said.

They had almost finished when one of the troopers patrolling the fort appeared round the corner of the stables. They all froze, Platt and Hebron looked instinctively towards Dirkman.

Although it was dark, no way could the trooper avoid seeing them. He said, 'Hey you, there, what're you doing?' Raising the carbine he was carrying, he stepped closer.

Platt's heart sank. The man was one of those self-righteous types, always willing to do his best, wanting to be promoted to corporal. No way would he be willing to pretend he hadn't seen them. He would raise the alarm.

'Oh it's you,' the man said, in his turn recognizing Platt and Hebron. 'I might have known. What the hell do you think you're up to?'

He got no further. He hadn't seen Dirkman hidden in the stable doorway.

As Dirkman quickly stepped up behind him, the trooper sensed movement but was too late. Dirkman brought his revolver down hard on the man's head and, with a little groan, he collapsed on the ground.

'Jesus,' Platt muttered. 'He ain't dead, is he?'

'No. I didn't hit him that hard. But, Charley, so what if he is? Others might have to be killed. Don't go soft on me.'

'OK, OK,' Platt said sulkily, wondering if there was a threat in the man's voice.

'Let's get this silly bastard outta the way. C'mon, Paul, grab his legs. Charley, finish saddling the horses.'

Together Dirkman and Hebron carried the unconscious trooper into the stables. They threw him into a far corner where he wouldn't be easily found.

'Shall we tie him up?' Hebron asked.

'No, ain't no need. By the time he comes to we'll be gone. The longer we stay here the more chance there is of someone else seeing us.'

'Warren? Charley ain't gonna let us down is he?'

Dirkman shrugged. 'I think his greed will get the better of any of his finer feelings. If not,' he shrugged again, 'he can be dealt with too.'

When they came out, Platt had mounted one of the horses and he held the reins of the other two.

'Let's go,' he told them.

Before anything else went wrong.

TWO

The stagecoach was late.

The small party of troopers waited in the shade of a stand of cypress pines. Beyond, the trail began its run across the valley floor before disappearing amongst a jumble of rocks on the far side. There was no sign of the stage, not so much as a rise of dust in the still air. The men were restless. Even in the shade it was hot, the sun a yellow ball in the cloudless sky, the slight breeze warm and brackish.

Mariner glanced at Colonel Gordon Woodford. Woodford was nearing retirement age. Mariner had the feeling with the way things were going at Fort Wilson the man was looking forward to it. Now he appeared worried, kept stroking his moustache which, like his hair, was white.

Not that it was unusual for the stage to be late. Mariner could hardly ever remember it being on time. So many things could happen. A landslip, cattle straying into its path, an accident, even trouble from Indians.

14

But what was unusual was that on this occasion other troopers were aboard, transporting the army payroll from Whipple Barracks at Prescott to Fort Wilson. Which was also the reason why Woodford was accompanying the patrol waiting to escort the stage the last few miles into the fort. Normally he would do no such thing, it being a long time since he'd ridden out with the troopers.

'Find out what's happening, Lieutenant.'

'Yes, sir.' Mariner jigged his horse over to where Sergeant Palmer sat his own animal. 'Any sign, Sergeant?'

Palmer squinted into the haze. 'No, Lieutenant.' The sergeant looked and sounded annoyed.

'What is it?'

Palmer obviously thought his position as a grizzled veteran of the Indian Wars gave him the right to speak his mind to a lieutenant he probably considered still wet behind the ears. 'I know the payroll is on its way, and believe me I'm looking forward to getting paid as much as the next man, but surely me and some of the men could've been spared to go after those damn deserters. I feel like I'm wasting my time waiting out here.'

Mariner sighed. Dirkman, Hebron and Platt. They'd run off last night. He knew he should have followed his instincts that they were up to mischief and done something about them yesterday.

'We could have caught 'em,' Palmer went on. 'It's bad for morale to just let 'em go. Others'll be thinking they can do the same.'

While privately agreeing, Mariner couldn't let his fellow officers down by criticizing their actions with a non-commissioned officer, however experienced he was. 'You and the men are needed here,' he said coldly.

'Yes, Lieutenant.' Palmer spoke in a way that showed how unimpressed he was.

Mariner turned to ride back to the colonel, then stopped and twisted in his saddle. 'Sergeant? Who was responsible for not sending those three out with Captain Johns?'

Palmer looked puzzled for a moment. 'I dunno. Platt was in the guardhouse but it wasn't for anything serious. He could've been let out a day or so early and the other two were available. When the orders were received their names weren't mentioned. Why, sir, does it matter?'

'No. I just thought it might have done them good to go out on patrol.'

'Yeah, it might. But those three would probably have deserted at some time or other.'

Mariner nodded agreement and rode back to Colonel Woodford. 'The stage isn't coming yet.'

'Umm.' Woodford pulled out his pocket-watch to stare at the time. 'It's rarely this late.'

'I know.'

'We'd better go and find it. Get the men ready to ride out.'

'Yes, sir.' And Mariner passed the order on to Sergeant Palmer.

*

'Watch out!' The frightened cry of the guard was loud over the pounding hoofs of the four stagecoach horses.

The driver looked up. Just beyond the bend he was negotiating the path was blocked by several large boulders.

'Oh hell!'

Even as Coombes hauled on the reins, he knew a moment of fear. They were going too fast, wouldn't make it . . . would crash. . . !

The air was filled with the squeal of the brakes as he tried desperately to slow the stage down. The horses whinnied as they veered out of the way.

A passenger cried out, 'What's going on?'

Someone else screamed.

With a tremendous bang the coach hit the rocks. The horses fell, tangled in their harness. There were more screams. The coach swayed first one way, then the other. It landed with a jarring thump and, as one wheel came off, spinning away, it veered along the ground, sending up a choking cloud of dust. Dragged to a halt by the horses and the harness, it tipped over on to its side.

Both guard and driver were flung from their perch to lie unmoving on the ground.

With triumphant yells, three men emerged from their nearby hiding-place and galloped down towards the coach.

And, suddenly, above the noise and the confusion came the sound of several shots.

*

It was deathly quiet when the patrol reached the scene of the accident.

'Oh my God!' Woodford exclaimed, bringing them to a halt at the top of the ridge. 'What the hell has happened?'

Below the stagecoach was on its side. Two of the horses were standing up, the other two remained fallen amongst the harness. Three bodies lay by the side of the trail, while others lay or sat in the shade cast by the coach.

Mariner and Sergeant Palmer exchanged a glance. Accident or deliberate? Mariner wouldn't have bet on the former seeing as how the payroll was on board. His fear was heightened when he made out that two of the bodies wore the blue uniform of cavalrymen.

As they galloped down the hill, the stagecoach driver stood up and limped towards them. He had a bloody cut across his forehead and more cuts on his hands.

'Thank God you've come!' he said in a high-pitched and panicky voice. 'I was afraid no one would. I didn't know what to do.'

'What happened?' Woodford demanded.

'We were attacked! We didn't stand a chance! There were three of the bastards. They just shot us down. My guard is dead.' Coombes's voice broke and he had to look away.

'How long ago?' Mariner asked.

' 'Bout an hour.'

'Umm,' Woodford said. 'Too long for those responsible to still be around. Lieutenant, don't just sit there. Sort things out.'

Mariner quickly started to give orders. 'Sergeant, see these people have something to drink. Try to right the coach. And put those two horses out of their misery.'

With a salute, Palmer immediately started to hand out his own orders.

Mariner dismounted and went up to the bodies. The guard's neck was broken, both troopers had been shot. He now saw that the other two passengers weren't badly hurt, had only cuts and bruises. The man, who was holding his head, wore town clothes, was obviously a drummer, while the girl had the look of an entertainer of some sort, which wasn't surprising if she was headed for Wilson.

Bending down in front of them, he asked, 'You folks all right?'

'It was awful,' the girl moaned. She wasn't very old and beneath her fear was quite pretty. 'I thought we were going to die.'

'We didn't know what was happening,' the drummer said. 'It seemed like it was just an accident until those outlaws rode up.'

The girl shivered. 'They just shot the soldiers. It wasn't even as if they posed a threat. They didn't have their guns out or nothing. They didn't need to kill them, did they? And they took my purse. Just snatched it out of my hand. They didn't need to do that either.'

As tears came into her eyes, Mariner patted her

arm in an effort to console her. 'Never mind, it's over.'

'And it's been so hot and uncomfortable waiting out here, not knowing if anyone was coming to help us. Thinking those men might come back.'

'Don't worry. They've gone. They won't be back. You're safe now.'

'Will you be able to get us to Wilson?'

'Yes, miss. It won't be long.'

'Thank God.'

Mariner stood up and looked round. It was clear what had happened. Here at the bottom of the hill, with more hills all round providing any number of hiding places for desperate men, an ambush had been set. And approaching fast, taking what was an easy bend, the stagecoach had run right into it. The driver would have seen it much too late to be able to do anything to avoid crashing. And in the following confusion the ambushers had struck.

Soon the stagecoach was righted, the men sweating and cursing in the heat.

'Come on, Sergeant,' Mariner said, and, with Palmer's help he began to search inside it.

They had almost finished when Colonel Woodford, who had been sitting on his horse a little way away watching all that was going on, rode up to them.

'Well?' he demanded.

'There's no sign of the payroll,' Mariner confirmed. 'It's been stolen.'

A ripple of dismay and anger went up from the troopers close enough to hear.

'Somehow I thought that must be the case,' Woodford said with a little sigh. 'And, Lieutenant,' he stroked his moustache, 'here are two troopers shot dead while doing their duty but where is the sergeant who was meant to be with them?'

'You don't think. . . ?'

'He was shot too,' Coombes said from behind the Colonel. 'But he was only wounded. He took off to see if he could follow the thieves.'

'Yes, sir, there, look!'

Mariner pointed to the top of the far hill. A figure in blue had appeared outlined darkly against the glare of the sky. As he made his way towards them they saw he wore sergeant's stripes and he was clutching his left arm where blood had turned the blue sleeve red.

THREE

United States Marshal Jubal Judd arrived at the town of Wilson in the middle of the afternoon. He realized as soon as he saw it that it existed solely for the troopers. Its one dusty street consisted of saloons, brothels and other places of entertainment where the men could spend their pay.

Not a great many people were around, most being indoors out of the sun. Those who were outdoors stared at Judd as he rode towards the fort, obviously curious as to who he was and what he was doing here.

Judd was quite used to people staring at him; rather liked it actually. He knew he made a splendid figure. In his early thirties, he was over six feet tall and broad shouldered. Curling down to his shoulders his hair was fair, matching his neatly trimmed moustache. His eyes were light brown. He wore black suits and white shirts, with colourful vests, while his boots started nearly every day by being highly polished. There was a small feather stuck in the hatband of his Stetson. A fancy leather holster supporting two Colt .45s was strapped round his waist.

If he knew that some people called him an ambitious dandy, he wasn't going to worry about it until they dared do so to his face. Something that was unlikely seeing how good he was with the Colts.

Although he was one of the youngest United States marshals in the West, he still wanted to do well; wasn't willing to sit back and let the deputy marshals take the chances and gain the commendations. The summons from Colonel Woodford had sounded urgent and as soon as he received it he'd started out. However, he might have thought twice about coming here himself had he known how hot and dusty the ride was going to be.

The fort was baking in the afternoon sun, the flag hanging limp from the pole in the middle of the parade ground. A quite large place, it had originally been built, Judd knew, to keep the area free from Indian trouble. Lately things had been mostly quiet and it no longer held the full complement of troopers. A slightly neglected air hung over it. The only two-storeyed building was the post headquarters, which also contained the colonel's living-quarters. There was Officers' Row, a large barracks, some one-roomed huts for the non-commissioned officers, and along one side several work buildings. They were all built of adobe and each had an overhanging porch, which provided the only shade, the rest of the fort being exposed to the brutal sun.

Not the sort of place, Judd decided, in which he would like to spend much time.

'Of course,' Colonel Woodford said as he waved Judd into a chair on the other side of his desk, 'I would probably have called in the Marshals' Service anyway because the payroll was stolen. But,' he shrugged, 'wouldn't you know it, after months of being quiet a few days ago we heard stories of Apache trouble down near the border. True or not,' another shrug, 'I had to send most of my men out to investigate along with my one and only scout.'

Although Judd hadn't heard the stories himself, the colonel's message had mentioned how the troopers were riding for the border. At first Judd thought he'd been summoned here to help find out what had happened to make the Apaches break out. Now he realized he was wrong. His help was needed with recovering the money.

Taking off his hat and placing it on his knee, and not wanting to waste any time, he said, 'Tell me about the payroll.'

Woodford frowned. 'It was coming from Whipple Barracks at Prescott. Just on thirty thousand dollars.'

Judd straightened. 'That's a helluva lot of money!' Surely much more than was needed for a place like Fort Wilson.

'I know,' Woodford agreed with a little nod. 'We haven't been paid for over three months now.'

That explained it.

'None of us,' he added in a discontented way. 'It's made things very difficult. Discipline is hard to maintain at the best of times. When the men haven't been paid for a while it's almost impossible. And the people in Wilson are getting impatient too and threatening to refuse to serve the men. Making things worse.'

'Why haven't you been paid for so long?'

'Oh no particular reason. Rumours of Apache outbreaks, troubles in various other parts of Arizona. You know the army, it doesn't need a reason.'

'There must have been a reason for so much money coming by stagecoach and not with an army escort.' Judd was incredulous. The army did some strange things but that didn't seem to make sense.

Woodford stood up, going to the window overlooking the parade ground and stared out. He rubbed his left shoulder as if it hurt and Judd vaguely remembered hearing how the man had been badly wounded in a fight with Indians soon after his arrival in Arizona. Clearly, at times anyway, his wound still pained him.

'That was Whipple's decision,' Woodford said as if he feared Judd was criticizing him. 'It was originally coming with an escort. But Whipple, like us, is short of men at the moment and when this Indian trouble flared up, it was felt their troopers were needed around Prescott. As the stagecoach has never been attacked before it seemed safe enough. And,' Woodford returned to his seat, 'it should have been all right. There were three soldiers on the stage. And

I was waiting with a patrol to escort them the last few miles into Fort Wilson.'

'But it wasn't all right?'

'No, I'm afraid not. Instead three people are dead and the money has been stolen.'

'Who knew about it?'

Woodford thought for a moment or two. It was as if he didn't want to tell Judd the army's business, even though Judd was there to help.

'A few people at Whipple. Those who made the decision I mean. The escort, who would have had to be told so they could get ready. And, here at Wilson, me of course and Captain Johns who is out leading the men to the border. That was all. Until the day before we rode out to meet the stage when I informed Lieutenant Mariner so he could get a patrol together. And I believe he told Sergeant Palmer. Palmer might well have told the men in order to reassure them they were getting paid, although he says he didn't, and so prevent any more trouble.'

'Trouble?'

'Yes. The night before the robbery we had three deserters. Hurt one of the other troopers during their escape. Not badly, thank God. I'm quite sure more of the men were ready to desert as well.'

'How were you told about the payroll? By telegraph?'

'Yes. We have our own telegraph here at the fort.'

'So the operator would have known?'

'Yes.' Woodford hesitated then leant forward. 'But

I'm sure he's completely trustworthy. He wouldn't
have told anyone else.'

'But he might have done so or someone could have
seen the message.'

'Well, yes, I suppose it's possible.'

'I'll have to speak to him.'

'I'm afraid you can't, Marshal.'

'Oh why?' Judd sounded annoyed as if he thought
the colonel was refusing him permission to question
his men.

'Because he's gone to the border with Captain
Johns.'

Judd paused. 'And you have no idea who the
robbers were?'

'No. We didn't see them of course and no one has
been able to give us a good description of them. I
suppose they must have come from Wilson. It holds
a number of the criminal element. They had obviously been plotting to rob the stage for some time
and just happened to strike lucky.'

Judd didn't look convinced. He didn't like coinci-
dences.

'What are you going to do, Mr Judd?'

'First of all I'd better speak to the sergeant who
was accompanying the payroll.'

'Sergeant Dell, yes.'

'Find out what he knows.'

'Very good. I'll ask Lieutenant Mariner to help
you. He's a bit inexperienced but otherwise capable.
He'll also show you where you can stay while you're
here.'

The orderly of the day was despatched to fetch the lieutenant. When Mariner came in, Judd stood up to shake his hand and saw he was almost as tall as himself. He had brown eyes and dark-brown hair that was cut very short. His uniform was brushed free of dust. Judd was a little amused to realize that Mariner, a career soldier, didn't consider Judd, long-haired and fancily dressed, to be his idea of what a United States marshal should be.

'Take Mr Judd to see Sergeant Dell,' Woodford ordered when the introductions were made. 'Fill him in on the little we know.'

'Very good, sir. It's this way, Marshal.'

Outside in one corner of the parade ground, some men were being taken through their paces by a sergeant, all of them looking bored and hot.

Judd was surprised when Mariner led him towards the guardhouse.

'I thought Sergeant Dell was wounded, not under arrest,' he said.

'He's not, not really. But it seemed best to keep him under guard until everything was sorted out. Just in case.'

FOUR

Sergeant Ian Dell was the only occupant of the guardhouse. He was locked in the furthest cell. As Judd and Mariner went in, he stood up and came to clutch at the bars of the cell door with his one good hand. That he wasn't best pleased about either his situation or their intrusion was no exaggeration!

He was in his late forties, a short, stocky man with iron-grey hair and eyes that seemed to stare into the far distance. His left arm was in a sling and beneath the suntan his leathery face had a pale tinge. He gave Mariner a smart salute while staring hard at Judd.

'Sergeant, this is US Marshal Judd,' Mariner said. 'He's here to investigate the payroll robbery.'

Dell didn't protest his innocence. Probably he'd been in the army too long to know that without proof that wouldn't do any good. He merely nodded.

'How's the arm?' Judd asked.

'It'll heal.' Dell had an Eastern accent.

'Good.' Pleasantries over, Judd went on. 'Tell me what happened.'

Neither did Dell say anything about having told his story several times already.

'I was escorting the payroll from Whipple with Privates Lock and Milne. Good men, reliable.'

'Did you know how much you were carrying?'

'No, sir, not exactly. But from the weight of the bags and the fact that Fort Wilson hadn't been paid for several months we knew it had to be quite a lot.'

'OK, go on.'

'The stagecoach was coming down a hill to a draw. Quite fast to help the horses pull it up the steeper hill on the far side. The driver knew what he was doing, had obviously driven the route numerous times.'

Mariner glanced at Judd and nodded.

'I remember thinking we should be at the fort soon and I could hand the money over to the C.O. But . . . one minute, fine. The next all goddamn hell broke loose. We heard the guard shout something out. He sounded scared. The next moment we hit some boulders placed across the path. The coach tipped over.'

'And then?'

Dell's face darkened with remembrance. 'Some men rode up. At the time I couldn't tell how many but the coach driver said there were three of 'em. They musta been hiding quite close by. They were firing guns. They fired at us.'

'That's when you were shot?'

'No, not then. Somehow I'd landed at the bottom of the coach. One of the other two passengers, a man—'

'The other was a young woman,' Mariner put in.

'Yeah.' Dell nodded. 'Well, anyhow, the man was more or less on top of me. I wasn't hurt but I couldn't move. We heard one of the ambushers clamber on to the coach. He pulled the door open. For a moment I thought he was going to help us.'

'But he didn't?'

'No.' Dell's knuckles whitened where he was clutching the cell bars. 'The goddamn bastard shot Lock and Milne. Quite deliberately.'

'But he didn't shoot you or the two passengers?'

'No,' Dell said again. He paused, waiting to see if Judd was going to make anything of that and when he didn't, went on, 'As you can imagine everything was confused. The girl was screaming. The male passenger cowered against me. Both of them thought they were going to be shot next. I couldn't do nothing. The bastard was joined by a second man. They tore the girl's purse out of her grasp and grabbed the bags containing the payroll.'

'Did you try to stop them?' Judd asked.

'Of course I goddamn did. Sir! And that's when the bastard shot *me.* In the arm. Then all of a sudden they were galloping away. And it went very quiet.'

Judd, who had been in a number of similar situations, knew what the sergeant meant.

'While we were struggling out of the coach, the

driver recovered and came to help. He told us the guard had broken his neck in the fall. He was real upset by it all. We placed the dead bodies side by side and while the driver made the passengers as comfortable as he could I tried to follow the trail of the killers. I didn't get very far. My arm was hurting too much, it was too damn hot and I started to feel faint. So I decided to go back to the coach and that's when I saw the patrol from Fort Wilson had arrived.'

Judd turned to Mariner. 'Did you go after the killers?'

'Yes, Marshal. Me and Sergeant Palmer. But the trail petered out in a line of shale and the men had long since disappeared. I daresay our scout could have followed their tracks but we couldn't. Anyway our help was needed with the coach and the passengers.'

'Right.' Judd turned back to Dell. 'Did you recognize the ambushers?'

Dell shook his head.

'Know 'em again?'

'I doubt it, Marshal. The two I saw wore long duster coats and masks. Had hats pulled low over their foreheads. I never even saw the third bastard and I didn't see their horses neither. Much as I'd like to, I can't help you.'

Judd couldn't think of anything more to ask the sergeant. 'Not right now anyhow but I might think of something else later on.'

'I ain't going no place.' Dell glared at Mariner as if the fact he was locked up was the lieutenant's decision and his fault. 'I should be out there doing something about catching the bastards. Lock and Milne were just doing their duty, they didn't deserve to be shot down like that.'

'What do you think, Mr Judd?' Mariner asked as they walked away.

'It's too early to think anything.'

'Do you want a word with the stagecoach driver, Mr Coombes? He's here in the fort hospital.'

'Yeah, all right.'

Hospital was rather a grand name for the small adobe building near post headquarters. But at least it was cool inside and clean. Three beds on either side of the room faced one another and there was a desk and chair between them. A captain sat at the desk. He was in his forties and his black hair was greying at the temples. Mariner introduced him as Captain Paris, the fort's doctor.

'Was Sergeant Dell badly hurt?' Judd asked.

Paris frowned. 'Not badly. I had to operate to get the bullet out. And he'd lost quite a lot of blood. But I'd say that if he wasn't under arrest he'd be ready to go back on duty.'

'He's not under arrest,' Mariner protested. 'Not really.'

'What about the driver?' Judd glanced at the man who lay on top of one of the beds, legs covered with a blanket. His head and both hands were bandaged. He had glanced at them when they came in and then gone back to examining the blanket as if he wasn't interested in anything else.

Paris lowered his voice. 'He's all right physically. But he seems very upset by his experience. The guard was a friend. They'd done the run together for a number of years.'

'Oh?'

'Yes,' Mariner answered. 'The stage is just a small line. It was put in specifically for the fort and Wilson is the end of the line. It only calls here a couple of times a week. There's not the custom for any more of a service. Any passengers are either coming here to the fort, to Wilson or they wait for another stage to take them further on. Coombes is the usual driver. I'm sure he can't be involved in this in any way.'

'OK, let's see what he knows.'

'It's the first time I've ever been robbed,' Coombes moaned. 'In all these years. And for those poor people to be killed at the same time . . . It's terrible. I can't believe it.' He broke off.

'It wasn't your fault,' Paris said.

But it was obvious others had told Coombes the same thing and he took no comfort from it.

And he couldn't add a great deal to Dell's story.

'I was thrown off the coach. When I hit the ground I lost consciousness for a while. I came to to find the three robbers were there, firing their guns, shooting my passengers. Believe me, mister, I pretended I was still unconscious!'

'So you didn't see what they did on the coach or the sergeant's reaction?'

'Not then, no, sir. But once the bastards had ridden away and I'd helped get the folks outta the coach, the sergeant was real angry over it all. Even though he was wounded he insisted on taking off after 'em. I said they'd be gone but he thought he could at least see the direction they'd taken.'

'What about the robbers, did you have a chance to see what they were like?'

Coombes shook his head. 'Didn't want to. I kept my head down.'

Judd didn't blame him for that. 'Did they say anything at all?'

'Not that I heard. Oh wait, yeah, there was something. Not much to help though. Just about how everything had gone to plan.'

'I wonder what they meant by that,' Judd said. But Coombes, Mariner and Paris had no answer for him.

FIVE

Somewhat to Judd's dismay, Colonel Woodford insisted on inviting him and Lieutenant Mariner to dinner. Judd had little time for socializing for the sake of it, especially with people he didn't know. He accepted reluctantly, knowing no polite way to refuse.

It was obvious that dinner parties at the fort were few and far between, for the colonel's wife had gone to a great deal of trouble. The table was laid with the best crockery and shiny silver cutlery. And the food had been cooked with as much imagination as could be given to beef stew and apple pie. The dining-room was situated at the rear of the post headquarters and looked out over a small garden in which some roses struggled to survive.

Hilary Woodford was a few years younger than her husband. She was a plump woman with blonde hair and pale-blue eyes and a dress that looked as if it should be worn back East and not on a fort on the Western frontier. Also present were Captain Paris and his wife and the wife of Captain Johns, both sensible-looking women, who had spent their married lives in places just like Fort Wilson.

Mariner had already told Judd that these three made up the fort's complement of officers' women. 'Although,' he added, 'they sometimes allow the sergeants' wives to join in with their activities. And Mrs Woodford makes sure everyone keeps busy.'

Now Hilary Woodford fussed round them all. As they sat down she said, 'So, Marshal, how do you like Fort Wilson?' Without giving him the chance to reply she hurried on, 'Of course, it is a little isolated. But we keep ourselves occupied as well as we can, don't we?' She beamed at the other two women, who smiled back not quite so enthusiastically. 'We have a weekly sewing-bee, quiz games and when it's safe we visit places around here. Accompanied by troopers, naturally, because it's never safe enough to go out on our own!'

Judd realized the woman was proud of her organizational skills and he wondered whether the others appreciated her running their lives for them. To give her her due, she was doing her best to provide entertainment in what otherwise must be a boring existence, and was, in fact, behaving as the colonel's wife should by looking after the officers' wives. But he bet her fluffy manner and little laugh got on their nerves!

Hilary glanced at her husband. 'Gordon is sorry so many precautions have to be taken, although I tell him we don't mind. He always wanted us to be stationed in Washington, which is where our eldest son is lucky enough to be, but somehow it never happened.' She gave a little sigh and touched her lips with her napkin. 'And it won't happen now as Gordon is due to retire in a few months' time.'

'I'm sure Mr Judd isn't interested in that,' Woodford interrupted his wife's flow of words.

She scowled unhappily at him. It was obvious to Judd that a posting to Washington, or some other civilized place, rather than one out here on the frontier – or rather the fact that there wasn't any such posting – was the source of many an argument between the couple. And everyone else was aware of the fact too, if their glances were anything to go by.

Woodford poured himself out a very full second glass of wine before offering the bottle around.

Judd, who didn't want to become involved in any domestic disputes, seized the chance to turn the conversation back to the robbery.

Eating the last of his beef stew, he said, 'Colonel, there were three robbers and the night before the ambush you had three deserters. Could they be one and the same?'

Woodford frowned, playing with the stem of his wineglass. 'Unlikely. How could they have known about the payroll?'

'Someone could have told them.'

'We've been through all this before, Marshal,' Woodford said somewhat crossly. 'Who could have told them? Apart from a very few people no one knew.'

'Well, I believe the thieves, whoever they were, were aware the payroll was on the coach.'

'You may be right.' Woodford sounded very disgruntled. 'That doesn't mean it was the deserters who were responsible. After all, according to Sergeant Dell the robbers wore duster coats and ordinary hats. Where would our troopers have got such clothes from?'

'They might have bought them or stolen them from someone in Wilson and then hidden them in the fort,' Paris suggested.

'Well that's possible I suppose. But even so I doubt whether the deserters could have carried out such a successful robbery. I'm told they weren't the brightest of men. Isn't that right, Lieutenant?'

Mariner nodded. 'True, Colonel, but . . .'

'But what?'

'Well, sir, one of the deserters, Charley Platt, came to us from Whipple Barracks.'

'Really? I didn't know that.'

'Nor did I until Sergeant Palmer told me.' Mariner spoke hastily as if fearing he might be in trouble with his colonel for keeping that information from him.

Judd sat up straighter. 'Where he would have known Sergeant Dell?'

'Oh, yes.'

'What do you know about the sergeant, Colonel?'

'Not a great deal.' Woodford glanced at Mariner and Paris, who both shook their heads; they didn't know Dell either. 'I've never served with him. But I do know he's been in the army a long while. Is a career soldier. And surely he must be trustworthy for the people at Whipple to allow him to accompany the payroll.'

'He is in the guardhouse,' Judd pointed out.

Woodford frowned. 'Yes, well, that was really just a precaution, not because I truly thought him guilty.' He frowned. 'I honestly cannot believe he's the sort to suddenly abuse the trust given him by not only stealing the payroll but killing two of his fellow soldiers.'

'Still you can never tell if other people's circumstances change or what they really feel. He might think the army owes him something.'

'The army owes most of its men something,' Hilary Woodford said with a laugh that made it sound as if she had drunk too much wine.

Judd saw the other two women look at one another with grimaces as if the wife of the commanding officer getting drunk wasn't an uncommon occurrence.

'And they don't go around robbing and killing.'

'We don't know Sergeant Dell has done that either, dear.' Woodford turned to Judd. 'I must admit when we first arrived at the site of the ambush I had my suspicions of the man, especially as he wasn't there. Instead, although he was badly wounded, he'd tried to go after the thieves.'

'Not badly wounded,' Paris put in.

And Judd said, 'What I can't understand is why should the thieves shoot two privates dead, deliberately, but only wound the sergeant?'

'Exactly,' Mariner agreed. 'Didn't you say something of the sort yourself, Colonel?'

'Well, yes, but now, I don't know . . .' Woodford
didn't sound pleased to be reminded of that and he
broke off without saying any more.

'Hasn't he a grown-up daughter who lives in Red
Rock?' Paris asked.

A town, Judd knew, midway between Fort Wilson
and Whipple Barracks.

'What's her name? Angela I think.'

'Of course I might be wrong and Dell be innocent
but I recommend an eye should be kept on him and
he shouldn't be released from the guardhouse until
I find out more.'

'All right, Marshal,' Woodford agreed reluctantly.

'What about the two passengers on the coach?
Any of you know anything about them?'

Shakes of heads all round.

'I suppose you questioned them at the time?'

'Yes,' Mariner said. 'They were both too scared to
remember much of what happened. As far as I know
they're still in town. Do you want to see them?'

Judd thought for a moment. 'No, I don't think so.
It seems to me more important to go after the
thieves. The longer I leave it the harder it'll be to
follow them and the further away they'll get. So
tomorrow morning I'll ride out to where the ambush
took place. See for myself what happened.'

'Good, good,' Woodford agreed. 'Do you think you'll
be able to follow their trail?'

'If the trail is still there I can follow it.' Judd was

reasonably good at tracking.

'You might be in luck. We haven't had any rain the last couple of days . . .'

'We never do,' Hilary mumbled.

'. . . and it hasn't been windy either. It depends on whether the thieves took the trouble to try to hide their tracks or just made a run for it.' Woodford paused to drink the last of his wine, then said, 'Take Lieutenant Mariner with you.'

Judd glanced at the young man. He preferred to work alone. He wasn't keen on having anyone else along, especially someone without too much experience. He knew better than to argue with the army, especially over an army matter.

'And, Lieutenant, you can stay with Marshal Judd until he finds those responsible or until he gives up the chase.'

'Yes, sir.'

Judd nodded and said, 'We leave early. Travel light.'

And Mariner, well aware what Judd was thinking, nodded as well.

SIX

It was getting dark when Dirkman said they ought to stop for the night.

'Shouldn't we keep going?' Platt asked.

'No, it's OK.' Dirkman grinned. 'I seen you looking over your shoulder. But there ain't no one coming after us. Not yet anyhow. We're safe enough.'

Platt had to admit the man was right, although he was unhappy at having it pointed out quite so bluntly.

'And there ain't much point in travelling when it's dark and we don't know what the goin' is like. We don't wanna have an accident, do we?'

They all giggled, remembering the accident to the stage. That had gone exactly as had been planned. It couldn't have been better.

'This is as good a place to stop as any,' Dirkman said with a glance round at the empty desert, which stretched flat and grey in all directions.

'There ain't any Apaches around, are there?'

This time both Dirkman and Hebron laughed at Platt's remark.

'Course there ain't,' Dirkman said scornfully and, as he got off his horse, added, 'Charley, see if you can gather up some brush, make us a fire.'

Platt looked down so the other two wouldn't see his scowl. Why did he have to do all the work? He bet that in the morning he'd be the one ordered to saddle up the horses, while they sat and took their ease. It had been the same at the fort. Dirkman was as fond of handing out orders as Sergeant Palmer. It wasn't fair. He also caught the glimpse Dirkman gave Hebron. They thought he was stupid and scared. Given a chance he'd show them.

A little later they were boiling up coffee and warming some biscuits over the fire to eat, which was so roughly erected it clearly wouldn't last the night.

Dirkman boasted, 'Y'see it was easy, weren't it? Like I done told you it would be.'

'Yeah.' Hebron, like Platt, had been surprised to find the payroll actually on board the stagecoach. He'd suspected it might be some kind of trick.

Platt looked at the bulging bags secured across Dirkman's saddle as if he still couldn't believe his eyes. 'Twenty thousand dollars,' he breathed.

His eyes gleamed. Twenty thousand dollars! It was more money than he had ever even dreamt of. More money than he'd hoped to see in a lifetime of hard work and harder knocks. Enough to live on for ever.

For about the first time he could remember Platt was happy. After a childhood of getting into trouble with the local law and then joining the army and getting into trouble with the sergeants, it was at last coming out right. Because now he was rich. He could have all the drinks and girls he wanted. Could do as he pleased.

All right, so they'd had to kill a couple of men to steal the payroll. He hadn't really liked that idea and was glad he didn't actually do any of the shooting. But, hell, at the same time, he didn't know the two troopers, they were strangers to him, who just happened to be in the way. And now it meant no more army, no more sergeants. No more *anyone* telling him what to do.

'What're you goin' to do with your share?' Hebron asked, knowing what Platt was thinking.

'Head for California and enjoy myself! I can't hardly wait.'

'Don't worry, Charley, won't be long now.'

'Hope not. I'll feel better once we cross into Mexico. Why can't we just go? I don't see why we've gotta keep our end of the bargain.'

'Because we have and that's all there is to it,' Dirkman said with a glance over at Hebron. 'After all, Charley, without that bargain we might have deserted but we wouldn't have got any money.'

'OK, OK, I know,' Platt said mutinously.

'And I certainly wouldn't feel happy to be always looking over my shoulder. Would you?'

'No,' Platt admitted, even while thinking it would

be impossible for anyone to follow all three of them in the vast wilderness that was Mexico, especially after they split up taking different directions. Sometimes Warren worried too much. He didn't dare say so.

Dirkman poured them out more coffee and feeling he should add a warning went on, 'But the law will be coming after us. And after what we done, it won't be just the army but a marshal or probably a sheriff. Someone who can track us.'

'Won't catch us though,' Hebron muttered.

Platt had known the risk he was running, known they couldn't rob the stage and expect to get away without being chased. But that was worrying. He resisted the urge to stare out into the darkness in case a man wearing a badge was about to approach them through the night.

'It just seems stupid to take chances we don't have to,' he moaned.

'There'd be more of a risk in not doing like we said we would,' Dirkman said. 'Don't fret, Charley, it ain't as if it's goin' to take us long. Coupla days is all. Anyway Paul's probably right. And even if the law does catch up there are three of us and we'll have surprise on our side.'

'We'll be more'n a match for anyone the law sends after us.' Hebron was confident. 'And after that we'll be home free.'

'Yeah, riding for the border,' Dirkman agreed. 'And to do that first off we've gotta get ourselves some new duds.'

It was all very well wearing duster coats but not much good when underneath were their old army uniforms. All the time they wore them, they ran the risk of being spotted and arrested.

'According to what we were told there should be a trader's store a few miles on. We can buy what we need there.'

'The trader won't cause us trouble, will he?' Platt said. He was fearful that they would be locked up and the army informed of their whereabouts.

'If he does, we can handle him.'

Hebron nodded. 'We can handle anything.'

'Yeah, but 'lessen he don't give us a choice we don't cause no trouble,' Dirkman warned. 'We're quiet and careful. No boasting. No showing him the money.'

'Warren, wouldn't it be a good idea to split the money up now?'

'No, best leave it till we get to Mexico. What's the matter, Charley, don't you trust me?' Dirkman laughed.

Well, no, Platt thought, he didn't, not particularly. He didn't see why Dirkman had to carry it all.

'We can stay the night at the store. Have something decent to eat. Rest up and then be on our way.'

Hebron said, 'Wonder if there'll be a gal or two there. I sure could do with enjoying myself for once.'

'I doubt there is.' Dirkman punched the other man lightly in the chest. 'Never you mind about that. You'll soon be able to enjoy all the girls you want! But the trader's bound to have a bottle or two.

We can have a drink. Celebrate. Eh, Charley?'

Platt nodded. He knew Dirkman and Hebron were laughing at him again because he wasn't very good at holding his whiskey. Got drunk after a couple of glasses. Perhaps they intended to get him drunk now and cheat him out of his share. He'd have to be careful, make sure that didn't happen. He'd also sleep with his gun close by; just in case.

Colonel Woodford left his wife tidying up in the dining-room and went upstairs to the bedroom. When Hilary joined him, he had pulled a chair up by the window, and was sitting, staring out on the dark night.

'What's the matter?' she asked, speaking carefully so as not to slur her words after all the wine she'd drunk.

Woodford turned slightly to stare at her. He too had drunk too much but he could handle it better. 'You realize I might be forced out of the army over this, don't you?'

Hilary came to a halt in the middle of the room. 'But, Gordon, why? It wasn't your fault.'

Did she sound concerned for him? Woodford didn't think so.

'I doubt whether the army will see it that way.'

'But you're due to retire in a few months. You've given them a lifetime of good service. Been injured through it. Risked your life on a number of occasions.'

Woodford laughed bitterly. 'Will that count for

anything against thirty thousand dollars? That's a lot of money for the army to lose. They'll want someone to blame.'

'Well, I don't see why it should be you.'

Woodford stood up, beginning to undo his shirt. He wondered whether she was being sympathetic towards him and his position or was thinking only of herself.

'Never mind, dear, you're always talking about wanting to go back East. I thought you'd be happy to return earlier than we planned.'

'Yes, Gordon, I do want to go home and return to civilization. I thought you did too. However, I don't want to go home in disgrace!'

He had his answer. And wasn't surprised by it.

SEVEN

Apart from the scuffed-up earth, there was little to show where the stagecoach robbery had taken place. A number of people had told Judd the robbers had set their ambush in an ideal spot. Now he saw that for himself. The driver would have seen the barricade of rocks much too late to be able to stop. It was a wonder everyone on board hadn't been killed.

'And you and Sergeant Palmer tried to follow the tracks over the hill?' Judd said to Mariner as he looked up at the scrub-covered slope. 'Why that way?'

'Well, partly because we first saw Sergeant Dell coming from that direction and he told us that was the way the robbers had gone.'

'So you only had his word for it?'

'At the time that would have been enough. But no,' Mariner shook his head, 'that wasn't all. It made sense. On our way here we hadn't seen anyone riding away in any other direction. Not spotted even a rise of dust. And whoever they were, the deserters or not, they would hardly have been likely to ride back towards the fort where they might expect to encounter a patrol. And this way,' he jerked his head towards the hill, 'is the direction to Mexico.'

'You reckon that's where they've gone?'

'Don't you?'

'Yeah, I guess.'

'Anyway, once we reached the top of the hill we made out the tracks of three riders. But we didn't get far before we lost them in the shale.'

'Let's go and look.'

The slope of shale was near the bottom of the hill. Although it extended for a mile or more and there were no tracks to be seen, it didn't take Judd long to find where they continued on its far side. He was helped by the fact that the deserters had dropped the purse they'd stolen from the girl passenger there; almost as if pointing the way.

He thought the only reason Mariner and Palmer hadn't found the tracks was because they were in a hurry to get back to the stagecoach. But if they hadn't been in a hurry and if they'd spotted the tracks then there would have been no reason whatsoever why they couldn't have followed them.

He mounted his horse from where he'd been studying the trail, wiped his forehead free of sweat, and said, 'It seems to me like they rode across the shale deliberately in order to slow down anyone coming after 'em, or maybe in the hope it would stop pursuit altogether. But now, see, they haven't made any effort at all to hide their tracks. They don't seem to be in any hurry either.'

Mariner frowned. 'I wonder why.'

'Perhaps they don't think anyone will come after 'em.'

'Surely they must.'

Judd shrugged. 'Who knows why outlaws do the things they do? If they acted like you and me they wouldn't be outlaws! At least it makes our job easy. But, Lucas, keep your eyes peeled and your hand near your rifle.'

'You think it's some sort of trap.'

'Maybe.'

But it wasn't. The trail continued easy to follow. It wound down through the hills and across a wide dusty valley, where the robbers had camped for the night, before entering the canyonlands, where it was hotter than ever. Always heading for Mexico. And they were catching up. Partly because Judd set a fast pace, partly because the robbers seemed to be ambling along.

Almost, Judd thought uncomfortably, as if they wanted to be caught. There was something about all this that he didn't understand and didn't like.

Towards evening of the second day they came to a halt at the top of a canyon. Below was a small trader's store: a long and low adobe building, with one door, one window, a flat roof and a corral out back, in which a couple of mules grazed on the sparse grass.

'Belongs to Trevor Kerwin,' Mariner explained.

'He was once a mountain man who drifted down to Arizona, married an Indian squaw and has stayed ever since. He's always been tolerated by the Apaches because he doesn't cheat them.'

As they approached the store the trader came to the doorway, watching them. He was quite old with leathery skin and grey hair reaching half-way down his back. And he bristled with weapons: a rifle held in one hand, revolver stuck in his belt, knife in his boot and another knife in a sheath under his arm. He looked quite capable of using them all. Willing, too, if he had to.

'He's not taking any chances is he?' Judd said with a grin.

Kerwin watched them ride round to the corral where they dismounted and left their horses. He watched them come back and enter the store. Only when he realized they didn't mean him any harm did he relax enough to put the rifle down.

The store was dark and cool. It was a welcome relief to go inside out of the desert heat. The room was divided into two: the store itself where counter and floor were piled with furs, tins of food and some farming equipment, and a bar with a table and a few stools.

Mariner wasn't so relieved to hear that the three men they were chasing were troopers.

'The deserters,' he said to Judd. 'Damn! I really hoped it wasn't them. And you,' he turned to Kerwin and demanded angrily, 'why didn't you do something to stop them?'

Kerwin cackled. 'Me, mister? Hell, I ain't been out here for thirty years or more without knowing when to turn a blind eye! It's kept me safe and my scalp on my head!'

It wouldn't be the first time deserters from Fort Wilson had come to his store, although he wasn't about to admit that to the snooty lieutenant. He dealt with them all, pretending not to notice their uniforms. Live and let live was his policy. Especially if they had money to buy what they needed. And in case they didn't, and expected to steal from him, he made sure he kept his weapons close by.

'There were three of 'em and they looked like they'd've been only too willing to put a bullet in my back had I asked any questions. So when they said they wanted to buy some duds and food you may be sure I said OK!'

'All right, all right,' Mariner said, putting out a hand to stop the trader's flow of indignant justification.

'What did they do?' Judd asked.

'Not much. Got drunk. Sat right there.' Kerwin nodded towards the table. 'One of 'em making sure his saddle-bags were next to the wall where I couldn't see what was in 'em. And they didn't say much of anything when I was in earshot. So it sure didn't take me long to tell they had something more'n deserting on their minds! They stayed the night sleeping it off and left the middle of the next morning. Didn't seem to be in any hurry. Tell you, I was glad to see the back of 'em.'

'Can you let us have some supper?'

'Bacon and beans?'

'Yeah. And we'll have coffee with it.' Judd had previously experienced whiskey sold at isolated traders' stores and he'd seen a still outside in the corral where Kerwin probably made his own. 'Maybe we'll stay the night as well.'

Outside the window the evening shadows were already spreading across the canyon.

Once Kerwin had gone Judd leant back in his chair and said to Mariner, 'So, tell me about the three deserters.'

'Warren Dirkman. I should say he's the ringleader in anything like this. Paul Hebron and Charley Platt.' Mariner frowned. 'I can hardly believe they are the robbers. Like the colonel said they never appeared clever or, rather, cunning enough to do something like that and not get shot in the process. And how did they know about the payroll?'

'Fort scuttlebutt?'

'Yes I suppose that's possible,' Mariner admitted reluctantly. 'The officers always think everything is a secret from the men. It rarely is. They usually know more than we do. And, of course, Sergeant Dell, if he is involved, could somehow have let Platt know. Thinking about it, I suppose he must have done.'

Judd nodded.

'It wouldn't be difficult. Visitors of all kinds are always coming to the fort. One of them could easily have brought Platt a message.'

Just then Kerwin came up with two tin mugs of coffee. It was strong, thick and black: probably not much better than his whiskey! 'Food'll be here real soon, folks.'

'Thanks. Go on, Lucas.'

'I don't know a great deal about them.' As a lieutenant, Mariner didn't know much about any of the troopers. Any orders or dealings with them were relayed through the sergeants. 'Platt hasn't been at the fort long. Only a couple of months.'

'And he came to you from Whipple?'

'That's right. Dirkman was with us the longest, just over a year. He's from the East. Hebron enlisted some nine months ago. I think he's originally from Texas and he drifted West before ending up here. Those two were already friends and when he arrived Platt just naturally gravitated towards them. They're all in their early twenties. A scruffy lot. Their uniforms never seemed to fit properly.'

Judd looked down to hide a smile. Mariner sounded annoyed. He was clearly a spit and polish type of soldier.

'And they weren't cut out to be soldiers. They were unwilling to take orders. Spent most of their time in the guardhouse. Or at least Platt did. The other two were too crafty to be caught very often. In fact, Sergeant Palmer told me he'd heard Dirkman and Hebron boast they'd only joined up in order to shoot Apaches!'

'They might not have found that so easy.'

'He also said Dirkman was offered the choice of

enlisting or going to jail back in New York where he was convicted on a manslaughter charge. I'd be willing to bet there were similar reasons for Hebron and Platt joining the army.'

'They wouldn't be the first.' Judd took a drink of coffee and grimaced. 'So it wouldn't come as too great a surprise to learn they'd be willing to shoot down two helpless men?'

'Rather than be caught, no, not really. You know, Mr Judd, the sooner the army stops recruiting these sorts of men the better, for everybody. They have no place in the modern army.' Mariner was very indignant.

'Why didn't they go out on Captain Johns' patrol?'

Mariner frowned. 'I don't know. I asked Sergeant Palmer the same thing and he didn't know either. It might have done them good.'

'It's perhaps what they thought they'd joined the army for.'

'Exactly,' Mariner said and shrugged. 'To be fair I guess they didn't think they'd be spending most of their time planting vegetables, making adobe bricks and doing pointless training exercises on the parade ground under a baking hot sun.'

'It hardly excuses what they did but I suppose it's an excuse for deserting,' Judd agreed.

'They certainly wouldn't be the first to run off. Mr Judd, do you think we'll catch them up before they reach Mexico?'

'Unless they suddenly put a spurt on, yes.'

'It's only about twenty-five miles to the border

from here. It won't take them long to ride there, however slow they're travelling.'

'Don't worry.' Judd didn't say anything but he had no intention of letting something like an international border stop his pursuit of the three men.

'Won't do you no good.' Coming up with their plates of bacon and beans, Kerwin had heard the last part of their conversation.

'What do you mean?' Judd asked.

'They weren't heading for Mexico.'

'No?'

'No, sir. Surprised me as well. But when they left here I made sure to watch 'em go. Didn't want 'em sneaking back on me. They went in the other direction.'

'And where does that lead?'

'Towards Red Rock.'

Judd and Mariner glanced at one another. Red Rock. That was where Sergeant Dell's daughter, Angela, lived.

EIGHT

Angela Dell let herself out of the two-roomed house she rented on the outskirts of Red Rock. Even though it was early, only just gone eight o'clock, it was already warm. It would be breathlessly hot for at least another month. The flowers she had planted earlier in the year were wilting and would soon need watering again.

She patted her fancy straw bonnet making sure it shielded her face from the sun: she didn't want to burn her skin!

Although she lived away from the bustle and noise of the town, Red Rock wasn't all that large. It wouldn't take long to reach Williams' Feed and Grain Store, where she worked. It, along with the livery stable, a barn and the stagecoach office, formed the business area. Main Street, with its stores, café, hotel and the marshal's office, was just round the corner. And beyond that was the red light district where, of course, as a decent young lady, Angela never ventured.

As she walked along, her high-buttoned boots echoed on the sidewalk. Quite a few people were about, anxious to complete their business before it got too hot. They all nodded and said good morning.

Angela smiled back. She liked Red Rock and her life there. Maybe the town didn't possess any of the refinements or elegance of the places back East she read about in magazines but it was a friendly town. Everyone knew everyone else. Neighbours were always ready to help one another. There was always something going on. And, despite the summer heat, she liked the desert. Strangers might think it dull and grey and uninteresting, she knew differently; it was always surprising and sometimes beautiful.

Moreover she enjoyed a great deal of freedom. Something, which as a young lady of twenty-three, she was sure she wouldn't have back East. Freedom was important to Angela. She didn't like following orders she didn't agree with or doing everything she was told. She liked earning her own living. She had a mind of her own and woe betide anyone who didn't think she should use it!

She let herself into the feed and grain store and went through into the back. Brad Williams wasn't anywhere around, although he had been by to open up, and she wondered where he was. As owner of the store he worked harder than any of his employees.

She took off her bonnet and shook out her light-brown hair which hung almost down to her waist. There was a lot to do, several orders to sort out, a delivery scheduled to come in later that morning and . . .

'Oh, Angela, there you are!'

She turned round to see Brad Williams standing in the doorway. He looked worried, his hair sticking up on end, and he was out of breath as if he'd been hurrying, something he seldom did.

'What's wrong?' she asked, for some reason her heart turning over.

'Marshal Follett asked to see me in his office. That's where I've been.'

He hurried towards her, touching her arm so she knew that whatever this was about, it was about her, not him. He also looked as if he wished it was the marshal who was passing on the bad news.

'What is it?'

'He's just received a message from Fort Wilson.'

Not Whipple Barracks; not her father then.

'There was a robbery. The army payroll was stolen—'

But if that was all it was, then Brad wouldn't be so concerned. It had to be about her father.

'—and some people were shot.'

'Pa?'

'Yeah, he was one of 'em.'

'Oh no!'

'But,' Williams added quickly putting out a hand towards her, 'he wasn't badly hurt. He was wounded but is now recovering.'

'Then what's wrong?' Scared, Angela almost screamed the question.

'Well, Angela, the thing is,' Williams paused, then went on, his words coming out in a rush, 'your father seems to have been arrested for plotting the robbery.'

'What!' Angela's legs suddenly gave way and she collapsed on the chair. 'Pa? He can't be! That's absolutely ridiculous. He wouldn't.'

'How long we gotta stop here?' Platt demanded, sprawling out beside the fire on which a pot of coffee was boiling.

'Until Warren says otherwise,' Hebron said. 'What's wrong? We're safe here ain't we?'

They had set up an untidy camp in the rocks which gave the town of Red Rock its name, where they could overlook the valley below them and see what was going on in the town.

'It's hot. I'm hot. It's dusty and boring. We should be on our way into Mexico.'

Hebron wanted to tell the other young man to shut up moaning. He couldn't be bothered. Platt was one of life's moaners and worriers.

Instead he said, 'It won't be for much longer now. We've just gotta wait a while, see if a lawman turns up after us. Be better if one does. But even if he don't,' and personally Hebron, who had no respect for the law, thought that only too likely, 'he'll soon learn we've come this way to where Angela Dell lives. That's what really matters. I reckon Warren'll wait till tomorrow and then leave.'

'Tomorrow? That's hours away.'

But it didn't seem like they were going to have to wait that long. Even as Platt opened his mouth to object some more, Dirkman slithered and slid his way down from the vantage-point where he'd been watching the trail into town. He looked excited.

'Two riders are coming this way fast.'

'Could you see who they were?' Hebron asked.

'One's got a marshal's badge on his chest and the other's wearing an army uniform! I can't be sure but I think it's old Mariner. It looks just like the upright way he rides a horse.'

They all giggled at that. They considered Lieutenant Mariner and his West Point manners a figure of fun.

'Good.' Hebron scrambled to his feet and began to stamp out the fire.

'Leave that, it don't matter. Let's go.' Dirkman eased his gun in its holster. 'Get this over.'

Platt opened his mouth to say he was staying behind. He didn't see why he should risk being shot by going up against a lawman and a lieutenant. Quickly he changed his mind. Dirkman was determined to do this and he held the money. Platt didn't intend to let that out of his sight. He'd simply make sure he kept well back out of the way of the bullets.

'Do you want me to fetch my wife?' Williams asked, worried at Angela's white face.

'No, no, I'm all right. Tell me what happened. Quickly.'

'Marshal Follett couldn't tell me much.' Williams

spoke quietly, trying to calm her down, sensing Angela's anger and distress. He found it hard to believe himself, for while he didn't know Sergeant Dell he did know, and trust, Angela, as he'd once trusted the rest of her family.

'Is he at Fort Wilson?' Angela had picked up her bonnet and was running the rim through her fingers.

'At the moment, yeah.'

'I must go and see him. Help him sort this out.'

'Just what I was going to suggest. You could catch the stagecoach to Whipple and from there take the stage that goes to Wilson.'

'That's a long way round,' Angela objected.

'There's no other way I know of. Not much goes to Wilson, you know that.' Williams looked at his watch. 'If you catch the stage that leaves at eleven you should make the connection and not have too long a wait at Whipple.'

'All right.' Angela had no choice but to agree. Even given the freedom of the West, she knew she couldn't ride all the way to Fort Wilson by herself; even though she knew the way and considered herself perfectly capable of doing so.

'Look, why don't you go on home, pack whatever you think you'll need while I go on over to the stagecoach office and book the tickets for you.'

'Thank you, Brad.'

'And, Angela, stay with your pa for as long as it takes. Don't feel you've gotta hurry back.' Williams kissed the girl's cheek. 'I wish I could go with you.'

'Oh no, no, I couldn't expect it. You've got your business to run and your family to look after. Don't worry, I'll manage.'

'Come back here when you're ready and I'll have the tickets for you.'

As she hurried home, Angela's mind was in a whirl. There had to be a mistake. There must be. Her father was no thief. He loved the army and would never do anything to hurt either it or his career. Would certainly never be involved in helping to shoot down two of his fellow soldiers.

But, given the army, she also knew that no one in authority would take much notice of what she thought or what her father said. And she wondered how, if it was necessary, she would prove his innocence.

NINE

'Before we do anything else we'd better go and see the town marshal,' Judd decided as he and Mariner reached Red Rock. 'It's only polite to introduce ourselves and he might be able to tell us something about Angela Dell. Anyway, we need to find out where she lives.'

'All right,' Mariner nodded in agreement. 'This seems a nice town, doesn't it?' Red Rock had decent sidewalks, porches for shade and a variety of stores. 'I've never been here before.'

'Me neither. There's the marshal's office.' Spotting the sign hanging outside the building, Judd pointed to the far end of the main street, which was busy with riders, pedestrians and a few carriages.

The marshal's office was a squat, square adobe building with a small jailhouse at the rear. Inside it seemed crowded with a couple of desks and chairs. On their entrance the marshal looked up, eyes widening as he saw both an army lieutenant and a US Marshal. He was in his early forties and had a drooping moustache and long beard as if to compensate for a completely bald head. Overcoming his surprise, he stood up, holding out a hand for them to shake.

'Marshal. Lieutenant. We don't often see folks like you here in Red Rock.'

Judd introduced himself and Mariner.

'Marshal Follett. Sit down. Want some coffee?' The man went to pour out three mugs and as he did so he added over his shoulder, 'How can I help you?'

'Do you know a Miss Angela Dell?'

'Oh! You're here about the payroll robbery.'

'You know about that?' Mariner said.

'Heard just this morning. Rider came in with a message from Fort Wilson. As well as asking me to look out for the three robbers it also said Sergeant Dell was under arrest.' Follett handed round the coffee and sat down. 'And you're here to talk to Miss Dell? May I ask why?'

'We've learned the three robbers were deserters, one of whom knew Sergeant Dell when he was at Whipple Barracks,' Judd told him. 'And they were on their way here.'

'Here? Not Mexico? That's more serious then. I must admit I didn't take a great deal of notice of the message, thinking the robbers would be sure to be heading for the border.'

The marshal sounded upset and annoyed with himself but Judd didn't blame him. It was a natural assumption to have made. He and Mariner had done the same.

'And you think they've come here to see Miss Dell?'

'What other reason could there be?'

Follett frowned. 'I honestly can't see her being involved in anything illegal.'

'Maybe she isn't. But it's odd, isn't it, how the three robbers are headed to Red Rock where she lives, rather than riding for Mexico?'

'Yeah, I guess,' Follett was forced to agree.

'So, Marshal, have you seen three strangers in town? They're young men. Early twenties. Probably wearing duster coats.'

Follett shook his head. 'I can't say I've noticed anyone like that. Sorry. Strangers are always coming and going in Red Rock. It's that sort of town. It serves the ranching community so we see a lot of cowboys here, some who get a job and stay, others who drift on after a few days. Unless they cause trouble they don't usually come to my attention.'

'What do you know about Miss Dell?' Judd changed the subject.

Follett thought for a moment then said, 'She's a nice young lady. Hard working. Popular. She and her family have lived in the area since before my time. And I've never heard a word said against any of 'em.'

'She lives with her family?'

'Nope. Not any longer. They're all dead now. She's on her own.'

'What about her father? Know him?'

'Nope,' the man said again, shaking his head. 'He must've been to Red Rock to visit his family but I can't remember ever having met him.' He paused. 'What are you going to do?'

'I think we must have a word with Miss Dell. See what she knows about what's going on.'

'Can you tell us where she lives?' Mariner asked.

'Yeah. You go out beyond the business district and hers is the road that is almost opposite the feed and grain store. And Miss Dell's is the house almost at the end with a garden out front. You can't miss it.'

'She has her own house?' Mariner sounded surprised. 'She lives alone?'

'Yeah, that's right.'

'Will we find her at home?'

'Either there, Marshal, or at the feed and grain, which is where she works. She also knows about her father's arrest because I told Brad Williams, her employer, and he was going to break the news to her. Knowing Angela, she'd want to visit her father, try to help him. I would say she's probably gone home in order to pack so she can leave for Fort Wilson.'

'OK, we'll try there first.'

Looking worried, Mariner said, 'Miss Dell's surely not going to travel all that way on her own?'

'Yeah, I expect she is. Why shouldn't she?'

'It could be dangerous, that's why. I doubt whether the Apaches will come this far but you never know.'

'Apaches?' Follett asked. 'What Apaches?'

'Well it might not be true but haven't you heard that a group of Apaches is said to have broken out of their reservation?'

'No.'

Judd glanced at the lieutenant, who said, 'Are you sure?'

'Yeah, of course. We ain't heard nothing like that here. Are *you* sure?'

'No,' Mariner admitted. 'It might only be a rumour.'

'Where did such a rumour start?' Judd asked.

'Where do any of these rumours start?' Follett put in.

Mariner frowned. 'One day the fort was quiet and the next it was buzzing with the news.'

'So much so Colonel Woodford sent out a patrol?'

'Yes the very next day.' Mariner looked from one lawman to the other. 'You don't think it has anything to do with the robbery, do you?'

'I don't see how it can,' Judd said. 'Like Marshal Follett says, these rumours are always springing up. Even so it does seem a bit convenient that this time the rumour was responsible for most of the troopers being absent from the fort just when the payroll was coming in. And when the troopers at Whipple Barracks were also on alert and not available to act as an escort.'

He stood up and Follett said, 'While you're talking to Miss Dell I'll take a walk round town. See if I can spot three strangers.'

'OK, Marshal, and be careful. Two men have already been shot.'

'I'll remember that.' Follett sounded as if he didn't like being told how to do his job. 'I'll take my scatter gun, no one goes up against that.' He paused then said, 'I hope you're wrong about Angela and her father. I really do.'

As they left the office, Judd said to Mariner, 'The marshal seems to think Miss Dell can't be involved.'

'He could be wrong. After all a girl who has to work for a living might be tempted by a share of thirty thousand dollars.'

Judd hid a grin. Obviously young ladies of Lieutenant Mariner's acquaintance didn't have to go to work any more than they lived alone!

Angela's house was easy to find. From the outside it was neat and tidy and some flowers had been planted in the garden.

Judd and Mariner dismounted and tied their horses's reins to the picket fence. As Judd opened the gate, the door to the house also opened and Angela appeared, carrying a bag. Judd heard Mariner catch his breath; well she was an extremely good-looking girl with a nice figure, shown off by the plain travelling-outfit she wore.

She stopped when she saw them, eyes betraying both surprise and a certain amount of anger.

'Miss Dell, we're here about the robbery . . .' Judd began.

She interrupted him. 'You'd better come in then. But I haven't got long. I'm catching the eleven o'clock stage to Whipple Barracks.'

As they went into the house, none of them saw the three riders at the end of the street, where they were hiding, watching. Waiting for their chance.

TEN

The inside of Angela's house was as neat and tidy as the garden. But she made it clear to Judd and Mariner that they weren't going to stay long enough to appreciate it. For she didn't invite them to sit down nor did she sit herself but stood in the middle of the room, bag at her feet, facing them with hostile eyes.

'We're sorry about this, Miss Dell,' Judd said. 'We just need to ask you a few questions.'

'About the payroll robbery?'

'Yes.'

'I suppose you think my father was involved?' Angela gave them no chance to reply but hurried on, 'That can be the only reason for you coming here. Well, let me tell you, you're wrong. My father is not guilty. And I'm on my way to see the commanding officer at Fort Wilson to clear this matter up!'

Somehow Judd managed to interrupt this tirade. 'Then why are the three robbers on their way here to Red Rock? In fact they've probably already arrived.'

Angela looked at him in surprise and shook her head. 'I don't know anything about that.'

'Have you seen them?'

'Of course I haven't! Why should I have?'

'Why else would they come here but to see you?' Mariner put in.

'I don't know!'

Mariner went on, 'Privates Dirkman, Hebron and Platt. Do their names mean anything to you?'

'No! I've never heard of them.' Angela's hands were clenched into white-knuckled fists. 'Why don't you believe me?'

'Don't you think it seems a little strange they're coming here?'

'Well, yes. And I don't understand why they should. But they're *not* coming to see me. They're certainly not bringing me any proceeds from the robbery! I can't tell you something I know nothing about. You've had a wasted journey. Now, why don't you leave me alone? Let me be on my way.'

Mariner looked as if he was about to continue arguing with the girl until Judd gave a slight shake of his head. They would get nothing more from Angela Dell. Perhaps she was telling the truth and she had no idea of what was going on. Perhaps she was lying.

The best thing, he thought, was to leave her alone; perhaps split up so he could go after the three robbers and Mariner could follow the girl, make sure she was, in fact, going to Fort Wilson.

'All right,' he said. 'Come on, Lieutenant, perhaps

we can accompany Miss Dell to the stagecoach office.'

Angela looked ungracious as if she was going to refuse his help but Judd was already headed for the door. He opened it and stood aside for Mariner and Angela to pass through before him.

Several shots rang out!

A bullet whined past Judd's head and slammed into the wall behind him.

Angela screamed.

'Christ!' Judd exclaimed, his heart leaping high into his chest.

More shots followed.

Judd half turned, shoving Angela hard. With a little cry she fell backwards, sprawling on the parlour floor. Judd ducked down just as another bullet thudded into the door by him.

Opposite Mariner had flung himself to the ground and was crouching in the doorway. 'Can you see them?' he yelled.

'Over there somewhere,' Judd pointed to the house on the other side of the road.

He managed to push himself through the door, yelling at Angela, 'Keep down!' Clawing out one of his Colts, he returned the fire with no real hope of hitting anyone, because there was no one to see. Their attackers were well hidden behind the wall of the house.

Beside him Mariner also fired a couple of times.

Judd reached out for Mariner's arm, dragging him in behind him and slamming the door shut. 'Everyone OK?'

Picking herself up from the floor Angela said in a shaky voice, 'Who are they? What do they want?'

Neither Judd nor Mariner answered her. Together they went over to the one window, opening the shutters a little way and peering out.

Judd glimpsed the glint of sun on a gun-barrel, saw a shadow on the wall of the house, a horse's rump. He counted the puffs of smoke from the guns. 'It looks like there are three of 'em.'

'The deserters!'

'Who else?'

'Hey! Hey!' It was Marshal Follett arriving at a run. He held his scattergun before him, looking as if he was quite ready to use it.

As he'd said, no one wanted to go up against that sort of weapon. Opposite there was sudden movement. Yells of fright and warning. Three riders came abruptly into view. While Mariner flung wide the shutters and fired at them, Judd raced to the door. He was too late. By the time he got outside they'd put spurs to their horses' sides and galloped away, quickly disappearing from view at the end of the road.

Angrily Judd stared after them. He considered giving chase but didn't. They were gone. For now.

'What's happening?' Follett asked breathlessly, coming to a halt at the gate.

'It was Dirkman and Co,' Mariner said, joining them and holstering his gun. And brushing down his uniform. 'I recognized them.'

'Hell,' said Follett. 'Are you sure?' He turned to Angela. 'Are you all right? Not hit?'

'I'm OK,' Angela said, shoving her hands behind her so none of the men would see how much she was shaking. 'I've never been shot at before.'

'I don't think they were shooting at you,' Mariner told her. Although he wasn't about to admit it, like Angela he'd never been shot at before and there was excitement and fear in his voice. And while it might have been better to keep quiet he found he couldn't.

'What does that mean?'

'Only that they were trying to kill me and Judd. Not you.'

'What do you mean?' Angela said again, her voice rising dangerously with both anger and reaction.

'All right, shut up the pair of you,' Judd ordered, before tempers could be lost. He was rapidly becoming in danger of losing his own temper because the situation was threatening to get completely out of hand.

It was unusual for there to be shooting in Red Rock in the middle of the day and in a respectable part of town. A number of people had quickly gathered to see what it was about, shouting excited questions. Brad Williams pushed through them all and hurried to Angela's side.

'What did they want?' he asked. 'How did they know you two were calling on Angela?'

'They must have been watching Miss Dell . . .' Mariner began.

'And why would they do that?' Angela demanded.

'They were waiting for us to turn up so they could try to kill us.'

Angela muttered something that sounded very much as if she wished they'd succeeded.

'They would have done as well if they were better shots.' For once Mariner was glad that Sergeant Palmer had never managed to teach the three privates how to aim and fire.

Judd decided it was time to take charge. All this argument was getting them nowhere, was only allowing the robbers to get further away. With Marshal Follett's help, he cleared the streets. Gradually the crowd drifted away still talking amongst themselves. Brad Williams refused to leave, he was determined to stay by Angela.

When it was again quiet Judd said, 'Lieutenant, I think it would be a good idea if you accompanied Miss Dell back to Fort Wilson.'

'Why?' Angela immediately said. 'Am I under arrest?'

'Of course not,' Follett said. 'She's not, is she, Marshal?'

'No,' Judd replied. 'But we might be quite wrong about what happened and Dirkman and the others were trying to shoot Miss Dell.'

Everyone knew he didn't believe what he said and that while Angela might not be under arrest he didn't want her to be left alone and perhaps able to contact the robbers.

Mariner and Angela glared at one another. Judd thought it quite likely they would spend the whole journey fighting. The alternative was for him to return to the fort and let Mariner chase the robbers, and he wasn't about to do that. The two of them would have to make the best of things.

Mariner looked no happier than Angela and he looked even unhappier when Judd went on, 'Rather than take the stage, if you ride that'll be quicker. That is, Miss Dell, if you can ride and you're willing to do so.'

'Of course I can ride,' Angela said indignantly. 'And somehow I don't think I've any choice in the matter.'

'Really, Marshal,' Williams spoke up. 'You seem to be treating Angela as if she's done something wrong.'

'I'm just taking precautions.'

'Well I don't like it.'

Angela put a hand on the man's arm. 'It's OK, Brad. I'll be fine.' She glanced at Mariner as if saying she wasn't in the least bit worried by him. 'It won't take us long to get to the fort and then all this can be sorted out. The sooner the better.'

'It might be best,' Follett added, also knowing from Judd's face that there was nothing any of them could say or do to make him alter his mind.

'I'll go and change into something more suitable for riding. Lieutenant, I own a pony. She's kept in the livery. Perhaps you'd go and saddle her for me.' With head held high Angela marched back into the house.

'God,' Mariner moaned. 'Mr Judd, this is not going to be an easy journey.'

'Never mind.' Judd tried not to grin. 'I'm sure

you'll manage. I'll start out after the robbers, this time they don't have much have a lead on me.' He sounded as if he knew he wouldn't fail to catch them up. 'And I'll join you back at the fort as soon as I can.'

'Do you want any help?' Follett asked. 'I know the country round here pretty well.'

Judd didn't particularly want anyone else along. All the same, someone with local knowledge might be helpful and allow him to pursue the men that much more quickly.

'OK.'

'Let's saddle up two fresh horses and get some supplies. Won't take long.'

Judd was anxious to be on his way but his horse had been hard ridden and he saw the sense of what the marshal said.

Together they strode off, leaving Mariner waiting outside Angela's house. Lucas frowned, wondering how he was going to cope, riding all the way back to Fort Wilson, with a furious and ill-mannered young lady along. He didn't want to be responsible for her.

He felt no better when Williams spoke in a self-satisfied way, 'She'll give you hell,' he said.

ELEVEN

'Pity we didn't kill 'em,' Hebron said when the three men came to a halt in the red rocks.

He would have liked to shoot dead a lawman – a United States Marshal no less – and a lieutenant; it would have been good for the reputation he thought he had. And he couldn't quite understand how they'd missed. It should have been so easy.

'Never mind.' Dirkman handed round the canteen of water. 'At least we've given 'em something to think on.'

Still anxious to reach Mexico and sure that this time pursuit wouldn't be far away, Platt resisted the urge to look behind him for tell-tale signs of dust. He said, 'We can head for the border now, can't we?' He hoped Dirkman wasn't going to suggest they set an ambush for their pursuers.

Dirkman didn't. With a grin, he said, 'Yeah, we can. And, Charley, just for you we can ride hell-bent for leather too! That way it should only take us a couple of days.'

*

This time the robbers were clearly thinking of escape. While they weren't doing anything to make it difficult to follow their tracks, perhaps, Judd thought, they didn't know how, they were travelling fast.

Marshal Follett said, 'Once we get beyond the rocks it's a straight run down across the desert into Mexico. It'll be hard going this time of the year but it won't take 'em long.'

Nevertheless Judd thought they would catch up, and soon. While they'd taken the time to saddle up two fresh horses, the robbers' animals must be becoming worn out by now. Would quickly become even more tired with the fast pace. And so long as they continued not trying to hide their tracks, he and Follett wouldn't have to take time out to stop and search the trail.

Follett glanced across at him. 'What's the matter, Marshal? You look worried.'

That's because Judd was. 'There's something about all this that doesn't seem right to me. I've thought so all along. I wish I could figure out what it is.'

'How d'you mean?'

'That's the trouble, I don't know.' Judd paused then seeing no harm in confiding his fears to Follett, went on, 'Why did the thieves come to Red Rock?'

'To see Angela?' Follett hazarded a guess. 'To give her her father's share of the money?'

'That's what we're meant to believe. And perhaps it's true. Yet both you and Williams are sure Miss Dell couldn't be involved.'

'Knowing Angela, no, it don't seem likely.'

'So why should they think she would accept a share of the thirty thousand dollars? Of course,' Judd added thoughtfully, 'she was leaving when we saw her.'

'Yeah. She was on her way to her father.'

'Or she was running off with the money.'

'Mebbe.' Follett obviously didn't believe that.

'Then there's the fact that me and Mariner were behind the robbers, by a half-day or more. They must have reached Red Rock long before us.'

'Yeah?'

'So why wait around until we arrived before going to see Miss Dell? If they hadn't, they could have given her Dell's share and been on their way to safety before we arrived. And so could she.'

Follett frowned in thought. 'Mebbe they knew you were on their trail and were waiting to set a trap for you.'

'But they could have done that anywhere,' Judd objected. 'Why do so in town where there'd be people to help us? By waiting until we were with Miss Dell it made it seem as if she and her father were involved.'

'You think it was done deliberately?' Follett frowned again. 'But if so why?'

'That's what I can't figure out,' Judd admitted. 'And who would persuade them to do something like that?'

'The person who told them about the payroll?'

'Then we're back to Sergeant Dell. And he would-n't deliberately incriminate himself and his daughter.'

'Hardly.'

Judd shrugged. 'Let's hope when we catch up with the deserters they can tell me all I want to know.'

Which seemed to say to Follett that not only did Judd not intend to fail but in succeeding it might just be that the three men would be shot dead. And he wouldn't be upset if so.

Mariner and Angela rode all afternoon without saying a word to one another. Angela seemed quite happy for it to be that way and every time Mariner tried to think of something to say he was all too aware of her animosity towards him. Any words he might have said died on his lips. And any effort on his part to act the gentleman and ask her if she wanted to stop and rest also seemed doomed to fail-ure. She was as good a rider as he.

Also, although he thought it unlikely the robbers would be following him and Angela, he was keeping a careful eye open for them. He didn't want to take any chances.

It was getting dark when they came to a slight draw in the desert.

'We'll stop here for the night,' Mariner decided.

He didn't really want to camp out all night with Miss Dell, it didn't seem right to him. But there was no alternative. They couldn't ride through the darkness. He cursed Judd for putting him in this position.

He drew his horse to a halt and dismounted. Before he could even think of helping Angela she had got off her horse.

He sighed and said, 'It's as good a place as any and will provide a certain amount of shelter. I'll gather up some firewood, start a fire. We can have something hot to eat and drink then. And we'll need a fire because it gets cold in the desert at night.'

He stopped abruptly, aware how formal he sounded and that from the scornful look on Angela's face she already knew all he was telling her; better than him probably.

All the same, as they sat on either side of the fire he'd built, and were drinking coffee, Mariner decided to try again. After all none of what had happened was his fault and Angela was an extremely pretty young lady, however sullen she looked at the moment. He wanted to be friends with her.

Nervously he cleared his throat. 'So, have you worked for Mr Williams at the feed and grain store for long?'

To his relief Angela replied, 'A couple of years.'

'I suppose you serve behind the counter, tidy up, that sort of thing?'

Oh, oh, somehow he'd said the wrong thing. He realized that as he saw her eyes flash in the firelight.

'No, Lieutenant, I do not serve behind the counter

or tidy up. I'm a clerk, responsible for keeping the account books, which Brad trusts me to do without any supervision.'

'Oh,' Mariner said helplessly. 'Sorry.' How could he have known that? He'd never met a lady clerk before. 'You must like it there.'

'Yes.'

A frosty reply and Mariner thought he'd made such a bad mistake Angela wouldn't speak to him any more. However, perhaps she felt lonely in the vast empty desert, perhaps she was scared of what she would find at the fort. For a little later when Mariner ventured to say, 'Tell me about yourself and your father', Angela drew her knees up and putting her arms round them said, 'I've lived near Red Rock all my life.'

'Oh? Yet your father is from the East, isn't he?'

'Yes, from near Pittsburg. When he was a young man he joined the army and was detailed out here. That was when he met and married my mother. She and her parents lived on a small ranch near Red Rock, which at that time was little more than a trader's store and a saloon.'

'It must have been a lonely life for her in those days.'

Angela nodded. 'Dangerous too. There was often trouble from Indians. The ranch house had a cellar and Ma could remember having to hide down there on a number of occasions while Grandpa drove the Apaches away either by shooting at them or giving them food. They had been married a couple of years when the Civil War started. Pa immediately left to fight for the North. Ma wanted to go with him but she was expecting me so Pa said it would be better, safer, to stay out here.'

'Even with Indians about?'

'Yes, because who knew what was going to happen in the East?'

'Where did your father serve?'

'I don't know. He never speaks about that time. Oh, he might have told Ma but he's not told me. I think he saw such terrible things he just wanted to forget them. As soon as it was over he came back out here to be near Ma and me. For a while we were happy together. Pa was soon promoted to be a sergeant and Ma liked being an army wife and I liked being an army child.'

'What happened?' Mariner asked for it was obvious from the way she stared into the fire that something had.

'Ma got sick and died. I was nearly ten. And I missed her oh so much. And it was so sudden. One day she was well, the next she was ill and a week later she died.'

'I'm sorry. It must have been awful for you.'

'Yes it was.' Angela blinked away tears. 'Pa decided he couldn't look after me and stay in the army at the same time so he sent me to live with my grandparents who still ran the ranch.'

'He didn't give up the army to be with you?'

Mariner was thinking only of her but it seemed he'd said the wrong thing again as Angela answered crossly, 'Of course not! He loved the life, which is why I know he's not guilty of any of this. And he knew my grandparents would look after me, that I'd be all right with them. Which I was.'

'What made you leave the ranch?'

'A couple of years ago both my grandparents also died. I couldn't run the ranch on my own so I sold up and moved into town. I'd already met Brad Williams and his family because we bought our feed from him. So when he offered me a job as a *clerk*,' she stressed the word, 'I accepted. And that's what I've done ever since. It's a good job. I get paid a good wage, the rent on my house is small and I have no reason whatsoever to want a share of a stolen payroll.'

'We'll be at Fort Wilson tomorrow. We can sort this out there.'

'I hope so.'

Angela's voice sounded bleak. Despite her air of anger and determination, Mariner realized how worried she must be. He wanted to go to her, take her in his arms. He didn't dare, fearing her reaction. He was afraid he was falling in love with her. Not just because of her looks but because she was brave and loyal. . . . But hell, afraid was the right word, because his feelings were hopeless when she obviously couldn't stand the sight of him!

'Best get some sleep now, Miss Dell,' he said with a little sigh. 'We can make an early start tomorrow before it gets too hot. With luck we should be at the fort by the early afternoon.' As he lay down he added as much to himself as to Angela, 'I wonder how Marshal Judd is getting on? I hope he catches those three.'

They could then tell the truth about the whole matter. He hoped for Angela's sake that she was right. But he had the idea she was very wrong.

TWELVE

With dawn no more than a pale streak in the eastern sky, Judd was awake and up, wanting to get on with the chase. Reluctantly he'd stopped for the night and now reluctantly he agreed with Follett to delay long enough to drink a mug of coffee. As soon as he'd finished he started saddling the horses.

With a sigh Follett threw away what remained of his coffee – he didn't see how Judd could drink it that hot! – and joined the marshal.

They took out along the trail and had ridden for an hour or more when Judd, slightly in the lead, held up his hand.

'Look! There they are!'

Three specks on the far horizon, but closer, much closer than they had been the day before.

'We should catch up round noontime,' Judd said. Then surveying the flat, featureless expanse of desert before them, he swore and said, 'But if we can see them they can spot us. They'll see our dust at

89

least. Make a run for it. They might even split up.'
Which would be the sensible thing to do.

Of course it wouldn't do them any good in the end
but it would make their capture that much more
difficult.

Follett took off his hat and wiped his forehead.
'Been thinking on that. If we go a mile or so out of
our way to the east we'll come to an arroyo. It cuts
through the land for several miles in more or less
the direction we want to go. I reckon if we ride along
it we could get within a short distance of the deserters without them spotting us.'

'Good. Let's go.'

The deserters were also up and riding early. Mexico
was in their sights. They were anxious to reach the
safety of the border.

Charley Platt rode at the rear, thinking, something
that didn't come easy to him. Three into $20,000 was
. . . it was . . . er, well, it was a helluva lot of money.
Enough for him to enjoy life. But . . . then . . . how
much more would it be if $20,000 was divided by two
or not divided at all? Twenty thousand dollars! All to
himself!

No, he shook his head, Dirkman and Hebron were
his partners.

On the other hand what did he owe them?
Nothing. If it had been up to him they would have
kept the whole $30,000. Would have crossed into
Mexico by now instead of going to Red Rock. It was
Dirkman who had insisted they keep their end of

the bargain, when Platt could see no good reason whatsoever to risk being captured or killed by doing so. Despite what Warren feared no one would have come after them.

And those two were the friends – look at them riding along together, laughing and joking, excluding him, treating him like he was a nobody or an idiot. It was as if they thought they didn't need him any more.

And if that was so, then perhaps they intended to cheat him of his share. Why else did Dirkman insist on carrying all the money in his saddle-bags? Why wait until Mexico to split it up? There was no real need to even go to Mexico. From here Platt was sure it was an easy ride into California, which, to his mind, would be just as safe.

The money should be his. Without him the plan wouldn't have been possible. Of course to get it would mean shooting the pair of them. He couldn't just rob them and expect to get away with it. Now *they* would come after him.

He didn't really want to kill them, had not yet killed anyone . . . but as Dirkman glanced round he was suddenly sure they meant to kill him. They had after all been quite ready to shoot the troopers. Platt waved and smiled back, pretending nothing was wrong, not wanting them to realize he suspected them, knew what they were up to. He had to protect himself. He could do it if he was quick and took them by surprise.

Couldn't he? Couldn't he? Could he?

*

The arroyo was deep, sandy at the bottom with steep rocky sides to which mesquite bushes clung. Easy going too. Sure the robbers wouldn't spot their dust, Judd kicked his horse into a gallop, Follett following close behind. Where the arroyo petered out, they left the horses at the bottom while they climbed the slope. At the top they wriggled forward, keeping low.

For a moment, Judd couldn't see anything and he felt a spurt of anger, thinking his quarry had escaped him. 'Where the hell are they?'

Follett touched his arm, pointing towards a stand of high rocks about half a mile away.

'It's them!' Judd nodded in satisfaction. 'And once they reach those rocks they won't see us. We've got 'em. Well done, Marshal!'

'You keep watch, I'll fetch the horses.'

Platt's heart was beating fast, his hands so sweaty he could barely grip his horse's reins. Could he do it? The words pounded in his brain. Shoot them? Steal the payroll for himself? Rather than have it stolen from him! It was such a lot of money, $20,000, that it was well worth the risk, especially when it wasn't a risk at all because they would never suspect him; not simple old Charley who didn't have an original thought in his head or any bravado in his body.

Yes, he would do it!

His chance came sooner than he'd imagined it would.

They were approaching a group of rocks which provided some shade from the sun's blast.

Dirkman said, 'Let's stop here for a while. The horses need a rest even if we don't. And there don't seem to be no one coming after us.'

Hebron turned in his saddle to look along their back trail. 'We musta given 'em the slip. Or else they've given up.'

Once they reached the far side of the rocks and were out of the sun, they came to a halt and dismounted. While Dirkman and Hebron fell to the ground, Platt remained by his horse, pretending to examine one of its forelegs. He glanced at the two men. As usual they took no notice of him, expecting him to look after the animals. Damn that! He was done with doing other people's dirty work. From now on he'd be the one giving the orders. He reached up, catching hold of his rifle, easing it from the scabbard.

'Hey, Charley, what you doing?' Hebron called. 'C'mon sit down, rest for a while.'

'You rest,' Platt muttered. 'For ever!' And clutching the rifle he swung round.

'What the hell?' Dirkman exclaimed. 'What the hell are you doing?'

'It's my money!' Platt yelled. 'Mine!'

'Shit!' Hebron swore.

It was the last thing he ever said. Platt pulled the rifle's trigger, once, twice. At that close distance even he, the despair of Sergeant Palmer, couldn't miss. Both bullets struck Hebron in the chest just as he was trying to get up. Blood spurted over his shirt. He collapsed back down, grabbing at the wounds, dying at the same time. It didn't take long, and he was quickly dead.

'Hell!' Dirkman rolled out of the way, scrambling to his feet and dragging his pistol from its holster. 'You sonofabitch!' he yelled, aiming at Platt.

Platt was scared. He'd made a stupid mistake. He should have shot Dirkman, the more dangerous of the two, first. Or waited until they were asleep. It was too late now. It was kill or be killed. He swung towards the other man and aimed back.

'Shots!' Follett exclaimed. 'What's going on?'

'Falling out of thieves?' Judd guessed even as he dug spurs into his animal's sides, sending it galloping forward. 'C'mon, let's find out.'

Dirkman and Platt both fired. Both missed. Platt dived for the safety of the rocks, throwing himself down behind the nearest one.

'We can talk about this,' he yelled in fright. 'Share the money two ways, Warren. You and me. It's what I meant all along. Think about it.'

Clearly Dirkman didn't believe him. He said, 'You think about this.' And fired again.

The bullet ricocheted off the boulder, sending chips into Platt's face, making him yelp.

'I knew I should never have trusted you, you snivelling little brat. We never needed you. Now I'm goin' to kill you like you done killed Paul!'

'Look! Look!' Platt saw the approach of the two lawmen. 'We're caught!'

Oh, hell, this was all going wrong. He'd never get to spend the money now.

At first Dirkman thought Platt was playing a trick. Then he heard the pounding of horses. And someone called out, 'Hold it right there!' He swung round, gun in his hand, lifting it towards his pursuers.

'Watch out!' Follett called in warning. He pulled on his horse's reins, veering out of the way.

Judd came straight on. His horse hit Dirkman, hard, knocking the man off his feet. As he dragged the animal to a halt, Dirkman came up on to his knees. He wasn't about to be hauled back to the fort to face a court martial. He would take his chances here and now. He fired.

Judd ducked the slug and, left with no choice, fired back. No way did he miss. His bullet hit Dirkman in the throat. The man dropped his gun and sank sideways, blood staining the ground red. He gurgled once or twice and was then quiet.

Meanwhile Follett had exchanged several shots with the still hidden Platt.

Seeing how hopeless his situation was Platt cried out, 'Don't shoot! Please. I give up.'

'Throw out your gun,' Judd ordered.

The pistol landed with a plop on the ground.

'And come on out, carefully! With your hands up.'

Platt did as he was told. While Follett kept him covered, Judd quickly leapt off his horse and patted the young man down, making sure he had no hidden weapons. He then secured Platt's hands behind him.

'What happened here?'

'Dirkman turned on us both,' Platt lied. 'He wanted the money all to himself. He shot Hebron. He was about to shoot me.' To his relief he thought the lawman believed him, or perhaps he didn't really care who shot whom.

'And where is the money?'

'In the saddle-bags.' Platt indicated Dirkman's horse.

Judd went over to the horse and hefted the saddle-bags to the ground. He undid the catches. All the money seemed to be there, still done up in neat bundles. But as he counted it out, he began to frown.

'What's wrong?' Follet asked.

Judd turned to Platt. 'You stole thirty thousand dollars. There's only twenty thousand here. Where's the rest of it?'

Platt grinned. 'Wouldn't you like to know?'

THIRTEEN

'Where do you think the money is, Marshal?'

Judd knew Follett wouldn't like his answer. 'Dell might have managed to hide it somewhere near the site of the ambush. But that isn't likely because then he'd have to find the opportunity to go back for it. So perhaps these three passed it to Angela before Mariner and me arrived in Red Rock.'

He glanced at Platt, longing to knock the smirk off his face, wondering what that smirk meant.

Follett frowned and didn't respond to what Judd had said. 'What d'you want to do now?'

'Let's get this one and the bodies back to town. Then I'll take Platt on to the fort. They can deal with him there.'

'And the missing ten thousand dollars?'

Follett wouldn't like what he was about to suggest either. 'I'd better search Miss Dell's house, see if it's hidden there.'

'OK. I'll help you.'

Judd felt Follett made the offer not because he

believed they would find the missing money but simply to keep an eye on him.

It didn't take long to sling the two dead bodies on their horses' backs. Judd prodded Platt on to his animal and they set off for Red Rock.

Once again Judd had the feeling he was missing something obvious. He'd expected Platt to act scared, to beg not to be taken back to the fort, perhaps offer the two lawmen a bribe. He hadn't. In fact he didn't even look particularly worried at the prospect of being charged with robbery and murder and facing a court martial. And Judd couldn't figure out why that was.

In the early afternoon Fort Wilson came into view. Mariner was pleased to see it, mostly because it meant he could hand responsibility for Angela over to someone else, but also it felt like home to him. However, he wondered what the girl riding by his side would think of it.

He felt he had to apologize. 'It's not much of a place, I'm afraid.'

'Don't worry, Lieutenant. I spent my childhood living in a frontier fort. I'm quite used to the lack of facilities.'

'It doesn't seem as if Captain Johns is back,' Mariner said as they rode past the guard, who saluted and looked at Angela with interest; the fort was as empty as it had been when he rode out.

'Where's Pa?' Angela demanded. Now they'd

arrived she wasn't interested in anything but seeing her father.

'We'd best go and let Colonel Woodford know what's happening first.' Before Angela could object, Mariner led the way to post headquarters.

With a mutinous scowl on her face, Angela allowed herself to be shown inside, where a few minutes later Woodford was free to see them.

Once he was introduced to Angela, Woodford sat with his hands steepled in front of his face and said, 'So, it was the three deserters who robbed the stage? And Marshal Judd has continued after them? Tell me, Lieutenant, do you think he'll succeed in catching them?'

Mariner nodded. 'From the little I know of Marshal Judd I should say that's very likely, sir.'

Angela said, 'May I see my father now?'

Mariner winced; Woodford was not used to being interrupted.

Indeed a frown of anger passed over the man's face but all he said was, 'Of course, of course, what am I thinking of, keeping you here? Lieutenant, perhaps you would take Miss Dell over to the guard-house?'

He made it sound as if Mariner was to stay with the girl and Angela's eyes narrowed. 'Colonel, tell me, am I, like my father, under arrest?'

Again Woodford looked surprised and a little annoyed at her forthright manner. 'No, my dear . . .'

My dear! Mariner's heart sank.

'. . . you are a guest here until this dreadful

matter is sorted out. I'll ask my wife to ready a room for you.'

'I'm free to come and go as I please?'

'Yes, my dear.'

As they left the office, Angela muttered something very rude about Woodford's patronizing manner. Mariner wisely pretended he hadn't heard.

When they reached the guardhouse she turned to him. 'You heard what the colonel said, so you can leave me now, Lieutenant. I want to see Pa on my own.'

'Yes, Miss Dell, all right.' Mariner touched the brim of his hat. 'Perhaps I'll see you later.' He hurried away before she could say something rude to that as well!

Dell, his arm no longer in a sling, still occupied the same cell. As Angela, smile fixed on her face, went inside, he stood up and said, 'Angela!' sounding very shocked to see her.

'Oh, Pa!' She flew to the cell, gripping his hands through the bars, all her determination to be bright and cheerful dissolving when she saw how tired and unhappy he looked. Tears slid down her cheeks.

'What are you doing here?' Dell blinked back his own tears. He added angrily, 'They haven't arrested you, have they?'

'Not exactly.'

'Well, they haven't arrested me exactly either but they obviously suspect me. I wasn't involved, Angela.'

'I never thought you were!'

'I would never do anything like that. Not rob the army nor be responsible for the deaths, no – murders – of two good men.'

'I know, Pa. It's all so stupid.' Angela paused to wipe her eyes then said, 'Pa, what happened?'

Dell told his daughter all he remembered of the stagecoach robbery and its aftermath. 'What about you?' he asked when he'd finished. 'Why are you here?'

'I had a visit from Lieutenant Mariner and a US Marshal.'

'Jubal Judd?'

'Yes.' Quickly Angela told her father her own story.

'And you can't remember the names of the three deserters?'

Angela wrinkled her brow in thought. 'No, Pa, I'm sorry. Lieutenant Mariner did tell me but I was so angry I never took much notice.'

'It doesn't matter,' Dell said, thinking that it might be important but not wanting to worry his daughter any more. 'But they were at Red Rock? They shot at Mariner and Judd?' He frowned. 'I wonder why.'

'That's what everyone said.'

'It can only be so they could pretend they were coming to see you and so put more blame on me. Nothing else makes sense.'

'But, Pa, why should they want to blame you?'

'I have no idea. But I wish I could get out of this damn cell and find out. No, no, Angela,' he quickly went on as he saw the look that came into his daughter's eyes. 'Don't even think of trying to break me out! It wouldn't do either of us any good.'

'If you're sure. . . ?'

'Yeah, I am.'

'Then I'll just have to find out for you.'

'What d'you mean?' Suspicion came into Dell's eyes; he knew his daughter, she was up to something.

'What I say. I'll investigate on your behalf. There must be some people I can ask questions of. Things I can discover.'

'You can't.'

Angela reached to kiss her father's cheek. 'Yes I can.'

'It might be dangerous.'

'I'll be careful.'

'I won't let you.'

'As you're locked up in here I don't see as how you can stop me. I'll see you later.'

'Angela!'

Her father's cry followed her as she left the guardhouse. She took no notice.

'Ah there you are, my dear.'

A fluting voice stopped Angela as she shut the door behind her. Another "my dear" she thought crossly. She turned to see a woman hurrying towards her. This must be Mrs Woodford, the colonel's wife. She was beaming as if Angela was highly welcome and not a disgraced sergeant's daughter.

'Welcome to Fort Wilson! I'm Hilary Woodford. My husband has asked me to prepare a room for you over in our house.'

Angela had been expecting to be put in with one of the sergeant's wives. Did the colonel want her close so he could keep an eye on her?

'It's all ready. Come with me. Then we can have a nice chat.'

Angela's heart sank. What on earth could she find to say to this woman, with whom she would have nothing in common, especially when she was eager to start proving her father's innocence? She curbed her impatience. She'd been riding in the desert for a couple of days now. It would feel good to wash away the dust and change out of her dirty clothes. And to rest for a while. So she smiled and allowed Mrs Woodford to take her arm.

And perhaps the colonel's wife was lonely and wanted someone new to talk to, for she sounded quite anxious to please as she went on, 'I hope you'll like it here. We don't have many ladies at the fort, more's the pity. But we're all very sociable. You'll be able to join in with our sewing-bees.'

Oh God! Angela thought. A sewing-bee! She who drew blood from fingers and thumbs every time she picked up a needle. No thank you!

When they reached Red Rock, Judd took Platt down to the jailhouse to get a deputy to lock him up, while Follett took the two dead bodies to the undertaker.

Afterwards Follett got the spare key to Angela's

house from Brad Williams, having to explain to the store owner why he wanted it. A furious Williams insisted on accompanying the two lawmen, standing cross-armed and scowling in the doorway, while they carried out their search of the house and Angela's few pieces of furniture. He wore a smug 'I told you so' look when they didn't find anything.

When they'd finished, Follett handed the key back to Williams, who made a big deal out of seeing them off the property and locking up behind them.

As Judd, not looking particularly happy at the situation, and Follett walked back to the jailhouse, the marshal said, 'What now, Mr Judd?'

'I'd like to stay in Red Rock overnight. But I really want to get back to the fort as soon as possible. If I set off now, I should be there late tomorrow.'

'Good idea. Marshal, do you want any help?'

Judd gave the man a disgusted scowl. 'I can handle Platt quite all right on my own. He won't be a problem.'

'What I really meant was what about carrying all that money?'

'No, I'll be OK.'

And Follett decided he would be. No one in their right mind would attempt to rob United States Marshal Jubal Judd!

FOURTEEN

Much to her annoyance, Angela had to endure dinner with not only Hilary Woodford but the other officers' ladies as well. Being questioned about her life and work. Patronized for being the daughter of a non-commissioned officer. Having to be polite for the sake of her father.

If she could help it she had no intention of suffering through another such meal. So she got up very early the following morning when the house was quiet and before, she was sure, the Woodfords were around. She washed and dressed carefully in plain skirt and matching jacket and boots and went downstairs and out into the still cool air. She decided to forgo breakfast, hoping to find somewhere in Wilson where she could buy something to eat.

Angela had almost reached the road that led to the town when a voice called out, 'Miss Dell! Wait!'

Damn! It was Lieutenant Mariner. He must have been watching the post headquarters. Why? Had Colonel Woodford told him to keep an eye on her?

Her suspicions seemed to be confirmed when, almost running to catch her up, he said, 'Where are you going, Miss Dell? So early too.'

'I was on my way into Wilson.'

'Wilson? Oh . . . but . . .'

'I believe the colonel said I was free to come and go?'

'Well, er yes . . .'

'I don't remember him saying that only applied to the fort?'

'Er, no.'

'So I can go into Wilson if I want to?'

'Yes, I suppose so.' Mariner sounded very doubtful. Wishing he wasn't always tongue-tied around Angela, he took a deep breath and said, 'I'll have to go with you.'

'Why?'

'Because it's not the sort of place in which a young lady like yourself should be left alone.'

Much as she wanted to argue with the lieutenant, Angela had seen exactly what the town was like when they'd ridden through it the day before. Annoying though it was, because she wanted to go there alone to begin her investigation and because she most certainly didn't want to be beholden to him, she had a feeling he might be right.

'I'll harness up a carriage.'

'I was going to walk.'

'No, Miss Dell, it's too far.'

'I'm quite used to walking.'

Mariner gritted his teeth, obviously wondering

why she had to argue with him over everything. 'Best not. There are no sidewalks or . . .'

'Oh all right.' Angela gave in ungraciously. 'I haven't got all day. We'll take a carriage!'

As they walked across the empty parade ground to the stables, Mariner said, 'Wilson isn't a very nice place. There aren't any stores.' He stopped abruptly as her face told him what she thought of being considered the type of girl who only thought of shopping. 'It's full of saloons and, er, and saloons.'

'I grew up near Red Rock when it was little else but saloons.'

'So, Miss Dell, may I ask you why you want to go into Wilson?'

Angela bristled, thinking it was none of his business. Thinking too that he wouldn't approve because he was the sort of soldier who always followed orders and toed the army line. And the army had decided Sergeant Dell was guilty. But as it was likely that once they reached the town he wouldn't leave her side, he would have to know sooner or later.

'I'm going to investigate the stagecoach robbery. Find out who was really behind it.'

Mariner's reaction was the same as her father's. 'You can't!' he exclaimed, sounding appalled.

'I don't see why not.'

'It might be dangerous.'

Exactly what her father had said. Did they both think she was a child who needed protecting or who wouldn't recognize danger and not avoid it?

'How can it be dangerous? The three robbers are over near Red Rock, nowhere near Wilson. And as far as you and everyone else is concerned you have the man responsible for planning the robbery in the guardhouse. So what danger can I possibly be in?'

'There's nothing for you to find out,' Mariner protested ineffectually, feeling the argument slipping away from him.

'I'll see about that.'

'I don't know what you hope to learn.'

'I believe there were two passengers on the stage?'

'That's right. How did you know?'

'Pa told me. He also said Marshal Judd spoke to the driver of the stage. But has anyone questioned the passengers?'

'Only at the scene of the accident. Not since, not as far as I know.'

'Why not?'

'I suppose it wasn't thought necessary. And Marshal Judd wanted to start out after the robbers.'

'They might know something important. Do you think they'll still be in Wilson?'

Mariner didn't know whether the man would be. He'd looked like a drummer. He could have travelled on by now. The girl, he was sure, had been heading for one of the saloons or brothels. He reddened. Angela couldn't possibly be allowed to see her. It wouldn't be right. The trouble was how could he stop her once her mind was made up?

*

Colonel Woodford came into the dining-room where his wife was laying out the breakfast dishes.

'Where's Miss Dell this morning?' he asked, taking his usual seat at the head of the table. 'Sleeping late?'

'No, dear. She's gone out.'

'What? Already? Where?'

Hilary was a little flustered as she always was when her husband treated her as he might one of his lowly lieutenants, demanding information from her. Something that happened frequently. 'Why, she left the fort. It looked as if she was going into town.'

'Into Wilson? What on earth for?'

'I don't know.'

'Didn't you ask her? Didn't you stop her?'

'I didn't think it necessary.'

'She shouldn't go there alone.'

Hilary looked relieved. 'Lieutenant Mariner was with her. She'll be safe enough. Why are you so worried?'

'I'm not worried,' Woodford barked. 'I was concerned for Miss Dell's safety, both on the road and in Wilson, that's all. Don't fuss. As Mariner is with her then everything is all right.'

But Hilary wondered if it was. To her mind, her husband still looked worried.

Much to Mariner's relief, when they reached the town, Angela seemed quite pleased by his company and didn't want to go off by herself. It was almost unknown for any nice woman to do any more than pass through Wilson on the way to somewhere else and Angela was quickly the object of curious eyes, not all of them over-friendly or polite.

'What are you going to do?' Mariner asked, taking her arm protectively.

Angela had thought of that. 'Speak to the clerk in the stagecoach office. He'll know if the passengers are still here, won't he?'

'He should do.'

'I'd also like a cup of coffee and something to eat.'

Mariner thought hard, and came up with a small café tucked behind a couple of the saloons on the edge of town. It was the only place where it would be possible to take Angela. It wasn't particularly clean, the food wasn't very well cooked but at least it was reasonably respectable.

'The stagecoach depot is on the way. We can call in there first.'

The stagecoach office was little more than a shack in the corner of the yard where the horses were changed. Luckily the stage was due that day so it was open for business. The man in charge was tall and scrawny with a full beard and clothes that looked like they didn't fit properly. Although surprised to be asked questions by Angela, he was willing to answer them.

'Yeah. Terrible day that were. First time the stage here's been robbed.' He turned to Mariner. 'Coombes ain't driving no more after what happened. He can't

face up to it. Can't say as I blame him.' Then to
Angela, 'Yeah, miss, there were two passengers
besides the three soldier-boys.'

'Are they still here in Wilson?'

'That they are. Man was a drummer. Selling all
kindsa fancies. He's in a room over the Silver Spur.
You're just in time. He's booked on the stage out
today. But it don't go 'til the afternoon so you'll have
plenty of time to seek him out.'

'And the other? A young lady wasn't it?'

'Wouldn't exactly call her a young lady.' The man
gave a little laugh before seeing the look on
Mariner's face. 'Er, yeah. Her. Name's Macie Finch.
She's a . . .'

'Sir!' Mariner cried.

'A working girl. Got a position in Madam Iza's, er,
establishment. Do you know it, Lieutenant?'

'I know where it is, yes.'

Angela glanced at Mariner who was very red-
faced. She almost smiled at his embarrassment.
Macie Finch wasn't just a saloon girl she was a prostitute, and Madam Iza's "establishment" was a
brothel. Well, she knew Red Rock had its share of
prostitutes and brothels. And she knew what went
on in them. She might not approve, and Mariner
might not approve of her talking to Macie, but that
wasn't going to stop her.

Judd woke Platt up by kicking him. He undid his
handcuffs only long enough to let him have a drink
from the canteen. Platt posed no threat whatsoever

but he wasn't going to take any chances where $20,000 of the army's money was concerned. He also decided that he wasn't going to waste time by stopping to have breakfast, not even coffee. They would have to make do with water and hardtack. The only time they'd stop would be when the horses needed to rest.

It was a long way to Fort Wilson but by travelling hard all day they should get there by the early evening. Then he could hand the money over to Colonel Woodford and be shot of Private Charley Platt.

That was something he couldn't wait for. Platt had done nothing but moan and groan – it was too hot, he was tired, they were riding too fast. Judd was becoming heartily fed up with his prisoner, almost wishing he'd escorted Miss Dell back to the fort and left Mariner to chase the deserters. Finally he'd shut Platt up by telling him that if he carried on moaning he'd gag him and tie him belly down over the saddle.

Platt had ridden quietly after that, all the time with a smug look on his face. As if he knew something Judd didn't.

FIFTEEN

Mariner was right about the café's shortcomings. The breakfast – weak coffee, greasy bacon and hard biscuits – was not only badly cooked but served on plates that needed washing. The floor could have done with a sweep. And the owner served them leering at Angela all the while, although she gave no sign of acknowledging him.

During the meal Mariner did his best to persuade her to give up seeing the passengers. He failed miserably.

'It's something I must do,' she said, and as soon as she'd drunk a second cup of coffee she stood up. 'Are you ready, Lieutenant? Let's go and see the drummer first. Just in case the stage should arrive early. I don't want to miss him. Do you think he'll be in his room or out trying to sell his goods?'

'I expect he's tried everywhere by now and that's why he's leaving.' Wilson wasn't that large. 'And he's probably in his room.'

'Then we'll go there. Where's the saloon the clerk mentioned?'

'The Silver Spur. It's at the end of the main street.'

'Will we have to go through the saloon?' Angela asked mischievously, smiling when Mariner reddened.

'No,' he said abruptly. 'There's an outside staircase.'

All the same they had to approach the staircase from the front of the saloon. Which meant approaching the saloon from the street. And the street was nothing more than other saloons, dance halls, billiard parlours and brothels. And the people in the street were nothing but bartenders, gamblers, drunks and prostitutes. Mariner was miserably aware they couldn't be mistaken for anything else. Thank God, he thought, at least it's daytime when not so much was going on.

He was also aware of Angela being stared at. If Angela was aware of it too, she took no notice. Please, he thought, don't let anyone say anything to us. Don't let them make rude remarks. At the same time he rather wished someone would so he could protect Angela and her reputation because by doing so he might impress her.

The Silver Spur couldn't be missed. It was Wilson's largest saloon and unlike the rest, which were of the rough and ready kind, had some pretensions to grandeur, with ornate lettering on the windows, glass in the upper part of the entrance door and a sign outside of a white spur against a black background.

The staircase was situated at its far end. It led to a balcony on to which several rooms opened. Mariner knew some of the rooms were rented by prostitutes and gamblers and he hoped their doors remained firmly closed!

'I wonder which room is his?'

So did Mariner. He didn't want Angela knocking on the wrong door; goodness knew what she might see!

'One of the bartenders will know. I'll go and ask.' He paused, frowning. 'Will you be all right here on your own?' He could see no alternative to leaving her alone. He couldn't take her into the saloon. But he didn't like it.

'You won't be long, will you?'

'No.'

'Then I shall be perfectly all right, thank you.'

'I'll be as quick as I can.'

'Yes,' Angela snapped.

Mariner was aware he'd annoyed her again. That she thought he was fussing unnecessarily. Couldn't she tell it was only because he was concerned about her? He hurried into the saloon and hurried out again. Much as Angela would never admit it she, sensing some of the strange looks she'd been getting, was glad to see him.

'It's the second door along. And as far as the barkeep knows the drummer, whose name is Mitchell, is in there.'

'Good.'

Mariner led the way up the stairs and knocked on the door. A few moments later it was opened by the man he recognized from the stage.

'Can I help you? Oh, Lieutenant, it's you. What do you want? Come on in out of the sun.'

The room was dingy and dark with nowhere to sit but the bed and one chair.

Mariner averted his eyes from the bed, which looked as if two people had slept in it, and said, 'This is Miss Dell. It was her father who was on the stage with you.'

'Oh yeah. The sergeant.' The man shook Angela's hand. 'Alan Mitchell,' he introduced himself. 'Sit down.' He swept some of his clothes off the chair. 'I'm just packing up. Now, miss, what can I do for you?'

'I'd like to ask you some questions about the hold-up,' Angela explained. 'I expect you know my father is suspected of being in league with the robbers. I'd like to prove he's not.'

Mitchell frowned. 'I'm not sure how I can help you. It all happened so quickly. And I'll admit I was scared. Not only over the accident, which was bad enough, but more so when those men rode up and started shooting.' He sounded a little ashamed.

'That was only natural,' Angela reassured him. She tried to hide her disappointment that he might not know anything. 'Do you remember much at all? Did there seem to be any connection between Pa and the three robbers?'

'Connection?'

'Yes. I mean did they act as if they knew one another? Did they speak to each other?'

'No, not that I heard. The two bastards, excuse my language, miss, but that's what they were . . .'

Angela nodded to show she didn't mind his language and hoped Mariner wouldn't say anything about minding on her behalf.

'. . . they didn't say anything. Or at least I don't think they did. They just climbed up the side of the stage, opened the door and shot the two private troopers before anyone could even think of stopping them. It was such a shock. And I thought we were all going to be shot as well.'

'I believe Dell was under you and couldn't move?' Mariner put in.

'That's right.' Mitchell nodded.

'That was convenient,' Mariner said, earning a glare from Angela.

'Oh no,' Mitchell said at once. 'That was because of the crash. It's just how we ended up. There's no way he could have arranged it on purpose. And there wasn't time for us to sort ourselves out before the robbers arrived. As you say, Sergeant Dell couldn't do anything, but, boy, could I hear him cursing under me. Sorry.'

He apologized again while Angela smiled; that was just like her father! Much to her mother's dismay she'd grown up learning a number of highly colourful words.

'And once the two men had snatched the bags containing the payroll—'

'How did you know it was the payroll?' Mariner asked.

'Well, I didn't then, of course. I've been told since.'

Angela frowned at Mariner, not wanting him to antagonize the drummer and stop him talking to her. 'What happened then?' she urged.

'Once the robbers had got the bags they disappeared. Straight off Dell pushed me out of the way. He clambered past the girl and the two dead soldiers. And he climbed out of the coach. And, miss, he jumped to the ground, shooting! He emptied his gun after 'em.'

Angela glanced triumphantly at Mariner. 'That certainly doesn't sound as if he was in league with them.'

'He didn't hit them though,' Mariner pointed out.

'They were already galloping away,' Mitchell said. 'They must have gone quite a way before Dell managed to get out of the coach.'

'And wasn't my pa shot by then as well?'

'Why, yes, miss. So he was. One of the bastards, sorry miss, shot the sergeant when he tried to stop him taking the bags.' Mitchell glanced at Mariner. 'I think that was a brave thing to do seeing as how they'd made plain their willingness to shoot to kill.'

'So do I!'

'As soon as the sergeant had helped the driver with me and the girl, he took off after the robbers. Of course, as he said, he couldn't catch 'em up but he could at least see which way they'd gone. And that was brave as well because if the robbers had seen him trailing them they might have come back and shot him dead.'

Mariner risked further offence. 'You didn't see Dell with any of the money? Then or later?'

'No.' Mitchell shook his head. He turned to Angela. 'I'm sorry I can't think of anything else, miss. Most of it is a blur. I don't remember it and I don't want to either.'

'You've been a big help.'

'I hope so, miss. You know, thinking on it I don't see how anyone could think your pa was involved with the robbers but I also don't see how I can tell you anything to actually prove he wasn't.'

As they left the drummer to his packing, Angela said to Mariner, 'There you are!'

'Like Mitchell said it doesn't prove anything.'

'It does to me. Pa was doing his duty.' Angela gave a little nod. 'And perhaps this girl, what was her name, Macie Finch, might know more. Now where does she work? Ah yes, Madam Iza's establishment. Umm, I wonder what sort of establishment that can be?'

SIXTEEN

Mariner came to a halt in front of Angela, stopping her, and, as firmly as he could, said, 'Miss Dell, you cannot go into Madam Iza's.'

'Why not?'

Mariner didn't feel up to explaining but just said, 'Because I will not allow it.'

Which naturally didn't go down at all well. Angela's eyes flashed angrily. 'Allow! What sort of word or idea is that? I didn't know I had to ask your permission before I did something.'

'It's not the sort of place you, or any other decent young lady, should go into,' Mariner said desperately. 'I'm saying it for your own good.'

'Lieutenant! I am well aware of what sort of establishment Madam Iza's is. And what goes on there. It's a brothel. And the girls are prostitutes.'

Despite her anger at his attitude, Angela almost laughed at the shocked expression on Mariner's face and his gasp of horror. He acted as if she shouldn't

120

even know such words existed let alone understand their meaning or be willing to use them.

'But . . . but . . .' he spluttered.

'I doubt very much whether I shall suffer any permanent harm by coming into close contact with such a place and such girls.' She might be shocked and upset, but Angela wasn't going to admit that.

'You can't.' Mariner made one last try. His protest sounded lame to his own ears. 'It's not right.'

'When my father's life and career are at stake, yes, of course I can. Now, Lieutenant, are you going to take me to Madam Iza's or should I ask one of these kind passers-by to show me the way?'

'Oh hell! You are the most. . . ! Come on.' Mariner gave up and grabbed her arm. 'It's this way.'

Madam Iza's was the largest, brightest and most popular of Wilson's brothels, for the girls she employed were young and pretty and the prices fair. As such it stood on the outskirts of the town in its own plot of land, with a strip of untidy garden at the front and hitching rails at both sides. It was a two-storeyed building with lots of windows, steps leading up to a covered porch on which were some seats, and an ever open doorway.

At this time of the morning, Mariner was thankful to see, no one was around. No horses at the rails; therefore no customers. No customers – so hopefully none of the girls would be in evidence.

He still felt this was wrong. All his upbringing told him so. A decent young lady shouldn't go anywhere near a . . . a brothel! He dreaded what his mother would say were she ever to find out. He dreaded what Colonel Woodford and Marshal Judd would say! He wasn't taking care of Miss Dell in the way he should. But it was all right for them. They weren't having to deal with Miss Dell! She didn't behave in the way the other few young ladies of his acquaintance did. And in his turn he wasn't sure how he should behave with her.

The door opened on to a large room, filled with several over-stuffed chairs, tables covered with fringed lace, crimson-red curtains and, although they weren't lit at the moment, candles and oil lamps standing on every available surface. Lilac perfumed the air. Paintings hung on the walls. Mariner hoped Angela wouldn't look too closely at them, although she could hardly avoid seeing the painting of the nude and rather rude girl wearing not even a wisp of lace, hanging over the empty fireplace.

Oh Lord! And, oh Lord, here was Madam Iza herself! Of whom, like most males in Wilson, Mariner was a bit afraid.

She was a tall, plump Mexican woman of indeterminate age. She had black hair piled in elaborate curls on top of her head, black eyes and very red lips. And an enormous bosom, most of which was revealed by the low-cut front of her black dress. She always wore black, a great deal of silver-and-turquoise jewellery and high-heeled shoes on which she tottered. She ruled her girls with a rod of iron but paid them well and protected them from difficult customers. So, although they had to work hard, they stayed under her roof at least for as long as they came up to her standards of youth and beauty, and enthusiasm.

'Why, Lieutenant Mariner.' She spoke in a husky voice that held only a trace of accent. 'It's very good to see you. Again.'

Mariner went very red and fidgeted uncomfortably. So, Angela thought in amusement, that was one of the reasons why he was so reluctant for her to accompany him into the brothel. He was one of its customers!

When Madam Iza spotted Angela her eyes narrowed. She recognized a respectable girl. She was afraid a respectable girl entering her place of work might mean trouble. The welcoming smile died on her face and she didn't sound at all happy when she said, 'I take it, Lieutenant, you are here on business not pleasure?'

'That's right,' Mariner stammered. 'We'd like to see one of your, er, one of . . . oh hell, Macie Finch.'

'And why is that?'

Again Mariner explained.

Madam Iza's expression softened a little. Although she hadn't seen them in years she remembered her own family with a certain amount of fondness. And now that she understood why Angela was here she was willing to co-operate. In fact, the sooner she did the sooner Angela would leave. Madam Iza hadn't been a respectable girl since the age of fourteen and she had no idea how to behave around one.

'I'll fetch her for you,' she said. 'Go on into the parlour. You know where it is.'

Stiff-backed with embarrassment, Mariner led the way into a room overlooking the garden. Thankfully it was empty. Angela sat on the edge of one of the stuffed armchairs while Mariner stood awkwardly by her side. In the circumstances, neither knew what to say to the other so they said nothing at all.

About ten minutes later, accompanied by Madam Iza, Macie Finch came in. She was a pretty, wide-eyed girl of around eighteen. It was obvious she'd been woken up, for her dark hair was tousled untidily around her shoulders and she wore a dress-ing-gown of red silk tied round her slim waist with a silk cord.

Angela had been a little fearful of actually meet-ing and talking to a prostitute, had thought she would feel superior and scornful.

Instead she experienced a pang of envy. Oh! If only sometimes her hair floated round her face like that and she could wear such bright, beautiful clothes! Instead of always having hair pinned tidily back from her face and wearing nothing but busi-nesslike clothes – like the jacket and skirt she had on today. Good quality, yes, but dark colours, plainly cut – boring! She felt boring!

She gave herself a mental shake. Surely it was better to be boring and have men respect her for herself rather than be colourfully pretty like Macie and be used by men? She saw Madam Iza looking at her with knowledgeable eyes and blushed, realizing the woman guessed what she was thinking.

'This is yours I believe?' Mariner handed Macie her purse.

The girl took it. 'Oh yeah, thank you! Those awful men stole it!'

'I'm afraid it was empty when we found it.'

Madam Iza muttered something nasty about what she'd like to do to those who would steal from poor working girls.

'Miss Finch, do you know of anything that could help my pa?'

Macie wrinkled her nose. 'No, miss, I don't think so.'

To Angela's surprise the girl sounded scared of her. Wouldn't meet her eyes.

'It was all so quick and I was real frightened. I hadn't ever seen a dead body before and then two men, who'd been talking and laughing with me minutes before, were shot dead in front of me. But, miss,' Macie added quickly as if she thought Angela might not like the thought of Sergeant Dell talking and laughing with a whore, 'your pa was real kind.'

'I'm glad.' Angela gave a little nod as if she didn't expect anything else.

'He helped me outta the coach and sat me on the ground. Made sure I weren't hurt. Then he took off after the bastards. I wish he'd caught 'em. I'm certain he didn't have nothing to do with the robbery. It came as much of a shock to him as it did to me.'

Angela hid a little sigh. Again there was no proof of her father's innocence. She doubted whether a court martial conducted by army officers would take much notice of a young prostitute thinking Sergeant Dell was kind!

Madam Iza suddenly said, 'It may be that you should look nearer to home for who was responsible.'

Surprised, both Mariner and Angela looked at her and Mariner said, 'What do you mean?'

'Just that you might like to ask which officer's been attending gambling games in The Silver Spur and who's lost a lot of money at 'em. Oh, I'm not talking about the gambling that goes on in the saloon itself. I mean the poker games held in the room at the back.'

'I've not heard of them,' Mariner said.

'No you wouldn't,' Madam Iza told him. 'You need money to get invited to play. We ain't got many wealthy men either here in Wilson or passing through but that's where the few we do have gather to play, once, twice a week.'

'And someone from the fort plays there?' Angela asked, eagerness in her voice.

'Yeah. And word has it he couldn't pay not just because the payroll was late but because the debt had run up to several thousand dollars.'

'That's a lot of money!' Angela said.

'Yes, miss. And certain people were getting anxious about being repaid. Threatening to go to the army command at Whipple.'

Which, Angela knew, would mean disgrace for the officer concerned.

'Who is it?' she asked.

Madam Iza looked first at Angela and then at the lieutenant, as if wondering whether she should say any more. 'I don't want to get into trouble.'

'You might as well tell us now,' Mariner said. 'I can always ask in the saloon.'

'Please,' Angela urged.

'All right,' Madam Iza made up her mind. 'It's Colonel Woodford.'

SEVENTEEN

'I don't believe her,' Mariner said, marching Angela away from the brothel. 'The colonel?' He shook his head. 'No.'

'I don't see why you're so unwilling to accept what Madam Iza said. You were quite ready to believe badly of Pa.' Angela was angry with him.

'That was different.'

'Not really.'

'Your father was in a perfect position to be the one responsible. He knew about the payroll. He knew Private Platt. He was actually accompanying the money.'

Angela stopped and, enumerating the points on her fingers, said, 'Colonel Woodford knew about the payroll and when it was arriving. He also knew Private Platt *and* the other two deserters. He accompanied you out to the stagecoach.'

'That was to lead the patrol,' Mariner protested.

'Was it? Or was it to somehow get his hands on his share of the money?'

'Of course it wasn't.' But Mariner said no more, remembering Colonel Woodford had ridden away while he and Palmer helped with the coach. Where had he gone? Why? No, no! It was ridiculous to think Woodford was a thief! He was the fort's commanding officer for God's sake. Lucas took off his hat and ran a hand through his hair. By God, he didn't like this. He wished he'd never become involved.

'Let's go back to the café, have some coffee and talk about it.'

Mariner wanted to tell Angela no, to order her back to the fort (as if she'd obey him!). Instead he followed as she strode down the road.

The café was as deserted mid-morning as it had been at breakfast time. The owner looked surprised to see them, as if amazed that someone who had once eaten his food was actually willing to come back for more! They sat at a table by the window as far away from the counter as possible so he couldn't hear what they said.

Angela leaned towards Mariner. 'Think about it, Lieutenant. Colonel Woodford gambles—'

'We've only Madam Iza's word for that.'

'Why should she lie? It's something that could easily be checked.'

Mariner waved a hand in the air. 'All right. So he gambles. He's not the only one. There's little else to do here.'

Angela didn't mention the girls at Madam Iza's. This wasn't the time for joking.

'He not only gambles, he loses, and heavily. And

the saloon-owner is getting impatient for the debts to be paid. Woodford can't pay. He's becoming anxious. Scared of what might happen. Scared of being found out. Then a telegraph arrives about the payroll and how it's coming to Fort Wilson in a few days' time. He immediately sees a way out of his problems. Steal the money and pay his debts. Probably have a little over to help with his retirement. You said he was due to retire soon, didn't you?'

'At the end of the summer.'

'But how to steal the money? He needs help. Who better than the three troopers on the post who would be only too happy to desert—'

Mariner interrupted. 'The colonel doesn't involve himself with the men.'

Angela tapped impatient fingers on the table-top. 'Maybe. But I'm sure he reads reports of who has been in the guardhouse and how many times. I daresay, with a little careful questioning, his orderly can tell him about those who would be willing to desert. I know I was only a child when I lived in a fort but even I was aware that there was little that could be kept secret. And I doubt whether deserters are a rare occurrence at the fort, are they?'

'No,' Mariner admitted.

'Next he has to see to it that there aren't enough troopers available at the fort to go after the deserters. And hopefully make sure that not many men from Whipple ride with the payroll.'

'And how does he do that?'

Angela looked at Mariner as if he was being

particularly dense and probably so on purpose. 'He starts an Indian scare. It would have been easy for Woodford to start the necessary rumours. Even easier to send Captain Johns and most of the men out to investigate them. And boy, oh boy, must he have been pleased when he learned that not only were most of the troopers remaining at Whipple, so the payroll was being escorted by just three men, but it was coming by stagecoach! His plans couldn't have turned out any better. Except that better still the sergeant in charge was Ian Dell who had known Private Platt at Whipple and they could easily be in league with one another.'

'What then?' Mariner asked, not really wanting to encourage her but caught up in what she was saying because, of course, she could be right.

'Somehow the colonel approaches the men. Says if they desert now they can rob the stagecoach which is carrying the payroll. He tells them what to do.'

'Someone must have done,' Mariner admitted. 'They weren't bright enough to work it out them-selves.'

'Right. He says it'll be easy. All they have to do is set an ambush. He knows a perfect place where the coach will be sure to crash. Surprise will be on their side. In return all he wants is his share. Which they can leave at the site of the accident.'

'Where?'

'I don't know,' Angela said impatiently. 'But I expect the colonel knew of such a place. He must have ridden the stagecoach route several times. It wouldn't have to be much of a hiding-place. Just a funny-shaped rock or a hole in a tree trunk. Somewhere the men couldn't miss and where they could quickly put the money and somewhere he could as easily recover it.'

'In that case Dirkman and Co must have stopped to count out the colonel's share,' Mariner pointed out. 'They could have been caught.'

'They'd surely have had time while those on the coach were sorting themselves out.'

'They wouldn't have known that for certain and it was still a risk. Someone could have seen what they were doing.'

'Then the deserters could have shot that someone as they had already shot the two troopers.' Angela shrugged. 'It didn't happen. No one saw them.'

'It would have been even easier if Sergeant Dell was in with them. Then they only had to wait on the other side of the hill and hand him the money.'

'And what did he do with it?'

'He hid it. Intending to collect it later. And no one saw him because he was able to order everyone else to stay behind at the stagecoach.'

Angela looked as if she wanted to hit him. It was lucky that at that moment the café-owner came up with their coffee and they were quiet until he left.

'The colonel isn't stupid. He would have known he was taking a chance the deserters would leave some of the payroll behind.'

Angela shrugged. 'Whoever helped them, and you said yourself they must have had help, was taking a chance. The deserters don't sound too bright. Perhaps they could be easily frightened into doing what they were told and who better to frighten them than the colonel?'

'You can't know that.' Mariner risked further displeasure by adding, 'And why did Dirkman and the others ride to Red Rock?'

'To put the blame on Pa. If Pa was blamed no one else would be looked for. Woodford could get off scot free.'

'Are you saying the colonel planned not only the robbery but everything else as well?'

'He could have,' Angela said stubbornly. 'Or maybe it was Platt's idea to put the blame on Pa and get his own back on him. After all, if he was in trouble with the sergeants at Fort Wilson it's more than likely he was in trouble with Sergeant Dell at Whipple Barracks.'

'Yes, I suppose so,' Mariner acknowledged.

'Although I still think it's more likely to have been the colonel's idea.'

'I can't believe he would agree to the shooting dead of two soldiers.'

'He might if he was desperate enough. Or maybe he didn't but the deserters shot them on the spur of the moment.'

Mariner paused to drink some of his coffee. 'Saying you're right, which I'm not, you understand, but if you are, how do we prove it?'

Angela sat back. She hadn't thought of that. 'I suppose we could ask in the Silver Spur. Find out if

Woodford has suddenly been able to pay his gambling debts.'

Mariner thought of the saloon-owner. 'I doubt whether he would tell me. He'd sooner tell me to mind my own business. With a few swear words thrown in.

'He'd have to tell Marshal Judd.'

'Yes.' Mariner nodded in agreement. A United States marshal could demand answers to his questions. And Marshal Judd would be only too willing to demand if necessary.

'Do you agree it's at least possible Colonel Woodford is responsible?'

'No.' But there was doubt in Mariner's voice.

Unfortunately, all Angela said made sense. Colonel Woodford was in a perfect position to arrange the robbery. And to be unable to pay large gambling debts might result in being dishonourably discharged from the service. Something Woodford naturally wouldn't want, especially when he was so near retirement and, as well as the shame, it might mean the loss of his pension.

'Lucas.'

Mariner's heart leapt into his throat. Miss Dell, Angela, had called him Lucas!

'What shall we do?'

Although he didn't want to appear indecisive in front of her, Mariner said, 'I think we ought to wait for Marshal Judd.'

'He might be ages.'

'Somehow I doubt it! Anyway I'd sooner wait and

place everything in his hands rather than act and do something he won't agree with. Miss Dell, I'm out of my depth here.' Might as well admit it. 'I'm a soldier, not a lawman.' That wasn't something to be ashamed of.

'Perhaps you're right. In the meantime it's going to be difficult to act normally around the colonel.'

'Keep out of his way as much as possible. I'll do the same. Meantime we'd better go back to the fort. We don't want Woodford to wonder where we are and what we're doing. And, Miss Dell, don't say anything to anyone about this.'

'Not even Pa?'

'Best not. Like you said, fort walls have ears. I don't want our suspicions, whether they're right or wrong' – and he hoped they were wrong – 'to reach anyone, especially the colonel.' Mariner didn't want to risk being dishonourably discharged either! He stood up, reaching for his hat. 'Let's hope Marshal Judd isn't long.'

EIGHTEEN

Nearly there!

Judd breathed a sigh of relief as he realized they were only a mile or two from Fort Wilson. He put some extra time on the journey by following a slightly longer route that wouldn't take him and his prisoner through Wilson. It wasn't worth taking the chance of meeting other troopers who'd known Charley Platt and who might take it into their heads to try and help him.

'What you goin' to do with me?' Platt asked as the fort came into view.

Judd had been thinking about that. It was the early evening, the sun was starting to go down. He doubted whether it was late enough for the men to be eating their supper. They would still be carrying out their last duties of the day. He hoped Colonel Woodford would be doing the same and would still be in his office.

He wanted to find out what was happening; whether Mariner and Angela had returned safely.

Most of all he wanted to hand over the payroll money to Woodford's safe keeping. So rather than lock Platt up in the guardhouse straight away, he decided to go to the post headquarters first.

When he told Platt so, Platt hid a grin.

'What shall we do?' Angela asked. 'It's getting late. I can't stay here much longer. The Woodfords will expect me for dinner.'

When she and Mariner had got back to the fort they'd decided she should wait out of sight in Mariner's home, while he carried out those duties he couldn't avoid. He'd returned to her as quickly as possible. The afternoon hours had ticked by oh so slowly but at least no one had been near or by. But now it was almost time for the evening meal. Neither could remain hidden for much longer.

'If only Marshal Judd was here,' Angela went on. 'He might be days away yet.'

'I'm sure he'll be back soon. In the meantime you'll have to go back to the Woodfords and pretend nothing is wrong.'

'I don't know if I can.'

'You'll have to. For the sake of your father. If Colonel Woodford suspects we've learned about his gambling debts goodness knows what he'll do.' Mariner still didn't wholly believe the colonel was guilty but being with Angela most of the afternoon he'd become affected by her jittery belief that he was.

'You're right.' Angela took a deep breath. 'In which

case I'd better be going.' She went to the door and opening it a little way peered through the crack, making sure no one was around to see her leave. She immediately slammed shut the door and turned back to Mariner.

'What's the matter?'

'He's here! Marshal Judd!'

Thank God for that! Now he could pass the whole problem over to the lawman.

'Are the deserters with him?' Mariner crossed to the window.

'One man is.'

'Only one?'

'Yes. And, Lucas, Judd is heading for the post headquarters.'

They stared at one another in dismay.

'And Colonel Woodford,' Mariner said.

Sergeant Dell was restless. He hated being confined. He felt he was going mad in his small cell. Especially now when he didn't know what his daughter was getting up to. There were times when he wished Angela hadn't inherited his stubborn determination. And this was one of them! He wanted to be out of here.

He went to the tiny barred window high on the wall behind him. If he stood on tiptoe he could see out. It was getting late. Already lamps were being lit in various places around the fort. The few troopers left on the post were preparing to eat supper and settle down for the night. Where was Angela? What was she doing? Why didn't she come and tell him what was happening? If she'd got into trouble surely someone would have been by to let him know? He'd have someone's hide for all this!

And ... Christ! There was Marshal Judd! And with him, a prisoner, one of the deserters. Dell wondered what had happened to the other two. Not that he particularly cared, not while there was one here able to tell the truth and so free him. As the two men came to a halt in front of post headquarters, the prisoner turned slightly as he went to dismount.

Private Charley Platt!

Dell smiled grimly. Now he understood. Platt. No wonder it was being made to look as if he was responsible for the robbery. And he wondered whether in fact Platt would tell the truth or would lie and say the robbery was all Dell's idea.

Platt's first posting had been to Whipple Barracks. It was soon obvious to a sergeant as experienced as Dell that the young man would never make any sort of soldier, let alone a good one. He could barely ride. He couldn't handle a gun. He was no use at following a drill. Nor were a lot of other green recruits. But Platt wasn't willing to learn or even try. Wouldn't follow orders. Surly, bored, feeling his punishments were everybody's fault but his own, he was forever being punished. They were both relieved when Platt had requested and been granted a transfer to Fort Wilson; where doubtless he was in just as much trouble.

Dell had heard how Platt had spent his free time boasting of his intention of paying Sergeant Dell back. Fat chance, Dell thought at the time. Now . . . well, Platt had clearly found a way of getting his own back.

Dell went to the bars of his cell. He had to get out of here, confront Platt. Force him to tell the truth.

'Hey, hey!' he called out. 'Let me out of here.'

But no one came to see what he wanted and although he rattled the bars they and the lock remained firmly in place. He could do nothing but wait.

'We'd better go and warn him,' Angela said. 'Judd could be in trouble.'

Mariner thought that normally Judd could handle any sort of trouble but he wouldn't suspect anything, wouldn't be on his guard. And this wasn't the time to protest that Woodford might be innocent. If he was nothing would be lost. If he was guilty then Judd might need help.

'I'll go. You stay here.'

'Why?' There was a flash of the old impatient anger in Angela's voice.

'Because it could be dangerous. There could be shooting. And while I know you're quite capable of looking after yourself I shall still be looking out for you. It might slow me down. Please, Miss Dell, Angela' – there, he'd used her Christian name! – 'don't make this any more difficult than it is already. I don't have time to argue.'

How would she take that? To his surprise Angela nodded agreement.

Having been shot at in Red Rock she had no desire to repeat the experience. Nor did she want to be in any way responsible for stopping Woodford's guilt and her father's innocence being revealed. Besides she had something else in mind to do.

'Be careful,' she said.

Mariner nodded and eased his pistol in its holster. 'If anything happens go to Sergeant Palmer. He'll know what to do.'

As soon as he'd gone, Angela slipped out of the house and headed for the guardhouse.

'Come on, you.' Judd pushed Platt into the headquarters building. 'Colonel Woodford in?' he asked the orderly. Receiving a nod he didn't wait for the orderly to find out if the colonel was available to see him but knocked on the office door and went in, Platt in tow.

Woodford looked up in annoyance at the interruption, opened his mouth to protest and then stood up abruptly when he saw who it was.

'Marshal! You're back!' He took a deep breath. 'And this is one of the deserters. I recognize him. Where are the other two?'

'They're dead.'

'Did you shoot them?'

'No. I haven't got the full story of what happened yet.' Judd glared at Platt. He grimaced. Platt still didn't seem in the least worried about being here at the fort, in the colonel's office. He was looking down at his feet, but that was to hide his smirk.

'What about the payroll? Where's that?'

'Here, sir.' Judd put the saddle-bags he was carrying down on the colonel's desk. 'I'm afraid I only recovered twenty thousand dollars. And I don't know where the rest of it is.' He hadn't managed to get Platt to tell him that either.

'I shouldn't worry,' Woodford said.

Judd glanced back at the colonel, alerted by his tone. Something was wrong here.

'I've got it.'

And before a very surprised Judd could do anything a gun appeared in the colonel's hand. And it was pointed right at him.

NINETEEN

'What the hell!' Judd exclaimed, taking an involuntary step backwards.

'Hold it,' Woodford said. He smiled. 'I shouldn't try anything, Marshal. You may be quick with those fancy Colts of yours but not even you can beat someone who's already drawn his gun.'

'I don't know what you're playing at—'

'Shut up! Surely it's obvious? I'm the one who helped with the robbery. But it's a long story and one I don't have time to tell you. I have an idea that Miss Interfering Dell and my infatuated lieutenant have found out some of the truth. Of course they can't prove anything because I haven't yet paid my gambling debts but they could be an inconvenient nuisance. So, now, Marshal, would you please release Private Platt from his handcuffs.'

Judd wondered whether or not to call Woodford's bluff. But one look at the man's eyes made him realize he wasn't bluffing; he would fire his gun. Judd cursed himself. Why hadn't he taken time out to think the whole thing through? He'd known something was wrong. Furious with himself and the situation, he unlocked the handcuffs. Platt stepped away from him, rubbing his wrists, grinning. It took all of Judd's self-control not to punch him.

'Thanks, Colonel!' Platt said cockily.

'Take his guns,' Woodford said sharply, clearly not trusting Judd wouldn't at least try and outgun him.

Platt did so, then, looking at the saddle-bags on the desk, said, 'What we gonna do now, Colonel? Especially 'bout the money. There's twenty thousand dollars there and no one else but you and me to share it.'

'Umm. By rights I suppose it's all yours. At the same time, with the way things have turned out, I've obviously got to leave the fort and the army rather sooner than I expected. How about I take five thousand of it?'

Platt frowned, unable to work out how much would be left.

Woodford said impatiently, 'That way we both get fifteen thousand dollars. It's more than you thought you'd have and if it's enough for me it must be enough for you.'

'OK.'

As the colonel began to count out the money, Judd said, 'You won't get away with this.'

'Ah, yes, and what are we going to do with you, Marshal?'

'Yeah, what?' Platt's eyes shone brightly with anticipation.

'I think we'll have to shoot him.' Woodford raised his gun.

The door was flung open. Lieutenant Mariner burst in, with the surprised orderly following close behind.

'Marshal Judd! Look out!'

Judd threw himself out of the way. The bullet from Woodford's gun exploded harmlessly in the wall behind him. Before Platt could think of firing one of the Colts, Judd launched himself at him. They fell to the floor, grappling together, trading blows and kicks. Judd quickly pinned Platt beneath him.

Woodford grabbed at the saddle-bags. He came round his desk and pointed the gun at Judd.

'No!' Mariner cried out. He darted forward.

'Lucas, don't!'

Woodford sensed the new threat. He span round and shot Mariner. The lieutenant was stopped in his tracks as the bullet struck him in the chest. It erupted out of his back, sending blood spraying over the walls. With a cry, Lucas clutched at the wound and toppled back, knocking over a chair, falling crumpled to the floor.

'Colonel, what. . . ?' the orderly said, having no idea whatsoever of what was going on.

'Out of my way!' Woodford yelled.

Wisely the orderly moved aside.

From somewhere above them came the sound of Hilary Woodford's anxious demands to know what was happening.

'Colonel!' Platt cried. 'Don't leave me. Please.'

Woodford took no notice. Didn't even glance back. He was gone.

Judd manhandled Platt to his feet. He took his frustrations out on him with a final punch that had Platt staggering. Quickly, he secured his wrists with the handcuffs again.

'See he doesn't go anywhere,' he snarled, shoving Platt towards the orderly. And telling him, 'You're going to the gallows, son. I'm personally making sure of that!'

'What is it? Where's my husband?' Hilary appeared in the doorway.

'And see to her as well.' Judd had no time to look after a wailing woman. 'Lucas. Are you all right?' Even as he spoke he could see that Mariner was badly hurt. There was blood everywhere and the young man wasn't moving.

Angela hurried to the guardhouse. She attracted no attention.

'Angela!' Dell exclaimed when he saw her, torn between relief that she was all right and anger that she'd been away so long when she must know he was worrying about her. 'For God's sake where have you been? I've been waiting and—'

'Yes, yes. Never mind all that.'

'I've seen someone I know. It's Charley Platt.'

'And I know who's really behind the robbery. Colonel Woodford. And don't look at me like that as if he can't possibly be responsible just because he's a colonel. He is. We've got to help Lucas, er, Lieutenant Mariner. I'm getting you out of here.'

'How?'

Angela pulled a pistol from the pocket of her jacket.

'Where did you get that?'

'I stole it from Lucas. Stand back.'

'Angela!'

She ignored her father's protest. She shot out the lock and the door to the cell swung open.

'Sometimes I wonder about you,' Dell said. 'Here, give me the pistol.' He took it and enveloped his daughter in his arms giving her a kiss and a hug. 'Are you sure about what you said?'

'Yes.' Angela was bouncing from one foot to the other in her anxiety. 'They're all over at headquarters now. Come on. There's no time to argue.'

But it seemed as if they would be too late because as they reached the guardhouse door, shots echoed from the headquarters building. And a few seconds later Colonel Woodford ran out. He leapt from the porch to the ground and caught the reins of Judd's horse. Mounting, he spurred away into the night.

'Quick!' Dell said. Followed by Angela he ran across the parade ground.

By now other troopers were appearing in doorways, demanding to know what the shooting was about. Wondering if it was an Indian attack.

Thinking horses might be needed for pursuit, Dell shouted at the nearest soldier to saddle up a couple of animals. Such was his authority that the trooper didn't hesitate to ask why a prisoner was giving out orders but hurried to obey.

Chaos appeared to have overtaken the post head-quarters.

Hilary Woodford was in the outer office, having hysterics, while the orderly, who still had no idea of what was going on, was trying to calm her down. A bruised and battered Private Platt was sitting in the corner. He scowled at Dell. His plans had come to nothing. All because of the treachery of an officer! He might have known. Life simply wasn't fair!

And in the colonel's office, Judd was bending over Mariner, trying to stop the bleeding with a piece of cloth torn from the lieutenant's shirt.

'Lucas!' Angela screamed, horrified. She pushed by her father to fling herself down beside the young man.

'Angela,' Mariner said in a fluttery voice and closed his eyes.

'The colonel's gone,' Dell spoke to Judd. 'We need to go after him.'

'You can't leave Lucas like this,' Angela objected. 'He might die.' Her voice rose to a wail.

'He needs the doctor, not us.' Judd looked up as other troopers crowded into the doorway. Among their open-mouthed surprise, he was relieved to see the older and wiser face of Sergeant Palmer. 'Fetch Captain Paris. Tell him there's a wounded man and a hysterical woman to look after. Get the other officers' wives to help Mrs Woodford. Hurry.'

'Yes, sir.' Palmer didn't stop to ask any questions.

Explanations could wait.

'Angela.' The girl raised tearful eyes to Judd. 'Keep holding this cloth on the wound. Tightly. Can you do that? The doctor will be here soon. He can look after Lucas. He'll be all right.'

'Are you sure?' Mariner looked very white to Angela, was having difficulty breathing.

'As sure as I can be. I've seen much worse bullet wounds than this and their victims survived.' Even if Mariner didn't do the same, Judd had to leave him, had to go after the colonel. 'Lucas was very brave,' he added, putting a hand on the girl's shoulder. 'He saved my life. Now your father and I must catch the colonel. You understand that, don't you?'

'Yes.' Angela nodded, reluctantly. 'Go on, go. And be careful, both of you,' she called after them.

Outside it was now dark. It would be impossible to follow the colonel's trail. But they would have to try because Judd knew Woodford would ride fast and hard, escape the one thing on his mind.

The trooper was bringing up a couple of horses. 'Here, Sarge.'

Across the way Sergeant Palmer was approaching at a run, Captain Paris hard on his heels. However worried he was about Lucas Mariner, Judd could, would have to, leave things in their hands.

'Good. Come on, Dell, let's be on our way.'

The two men swung up into the saddles and spurred the horses away from the fort. The night quickly swallowed them up.

TWENTY

As they headed the horses away from the fort, Dell looked across at Judd and said, 'It was hard enough to believe Colonel Woodford was behind the robbery. That he helped the deserters plan it. But that in escaping he should be willing to shoot one of his own officers . . .' He broke off, shaking his head, disturbed and upset by what had happened. 'It's beyond me.'

'I know. Me too.'

'Have you any idea why?'

'No, Dell, I'm as shocked by this as you. All I can think is that Woodford wanted something more than his army pension to retire on. Or thought he was entitled to more. One thing, he and his wife didn't seem to get on all that well so maybe that had something to do with it.'

They came to a creek and splashed across the trickle of water that barely covered the sandy bed. Beyond, the land stretched away into flat emptiness, any landmarks already hidden from view.

'Are you familiar with this region at all?' Judd felt

at a disadvantage because he hadn't been this way before whereas Colonel Woodford would know the area quite well.

So he was relieved when Dell said, 'Been here a time or two.'

'OK. Reckoning he'll try for Mexico, which way will he go?'

Dell thought for a moment. 'He heads across this valley, he'll eventually come to another creek. If he follows that for several miles he can then turn off into a few miles of canyonlands. After that the next valley leads more or less straight down to the border.'

'That's the way we'll go.'

'Supposing you're wrong?' Dell objected.

'Unless we wait until morning to follow his tracks, by which time he could have gotten so far ahead we won't be able to catch up, I don't see we've got much choice but to take the chance.'

Dell nodded agreement.

Angela sat anxiously by Mariner's side where he lay on the doctor's table. She held tight to his hand, not daring to ask how he was for fear of the answer, especially when Captain Paris had appeared worried by all the blood.

But Paris was relieved to find that the lieutenant's wound wasn't as bad as it had at first appeared. The bullet hadn't hit anything vital. It wasn't still in the wound. All he had to do was clean the entrance and exit wounds thoroughly and bind them up. Hope Mariner hadn't lost too much blood. And wait.

He glanced across at Angela's tear-stained face and tried to put her mind at rest. 'Don't worry. He's young and strong. That'll give him a good chance of recovery. But he will need a lot of care.'

'I'll help all I can.'

As Paris turned away to fetch some bandages, Mariner's eyes flickered open.

'Angela.' His voice was a croak.

'Yes, I'm here.' She stroked his hair away from his forehead.

'I hurt.'

'You'll be fine. The doctor says so. He's going to bandage you up and then put you to bed.'

'Will you stay with me?'

'Of course I will.'

'Angela.' Mariner's voice was fading as he drifted back into unconsciousness and she had to bend over him to hear what he said, 'I love you. Do you think you can ever come to love me?'

Angela smiled. Before she could say anything he had closed his eyes and was asleep. She kissed his lips lightly hoping he would somehow know her answer. She had liked the army life when she was a child. She had always dreamt of being an army wife.

Woodford came to a halt. His horse needed to rest if it was going to take him all the way into Mexico. But he was reluctant to stop because pursuit was inevitable, especially when the likes of Marshal Judd was involved.

Why, oh why, had he asked for help from the United States Marshals' Service, even though it would have looked strange if he hadn't? He'd hoped that the marshal would be fooled into thinking Sergeant Dell was involved with the robbers and so not look elsewhere for the real culprit. Now he thought how stupid that was. A man didn't get to become a United States Marshal by being easily deceived.

His one hope now was that events at the fort had delayed those coming after him. Despite his situation, he couldn't help but grin, thinking about people's reactions: at their shock as they realized the colonel, their commanding officer, was not only an unsuccessful gambler but also a thief, willing to shoot an officer rather than be arrested. It was a shame about Lieutenant Mariner but the stupid fool should have minded his own business, not got in the way. He didn't even wonder about Charley Platt, languishing in the guardhouse. A mere private was not worth his bothering over.

But as he thought of Hilary and her shame and rage he grinned even wider. What would she do? He didn't care. It served her right for always reminding him he was a failure for not being transferred to Washington. And what would the army say? Well, the army had never done much for him. Hadn't agreed to his many requests for transfer to an easier post, even after he was badly wounded in the line of duty. Had expected him to carry on.

Things hadn't exactly gone according to his plan. He'd wanted to see out his remaining months in the army, receive his pension and go back East. But on reflection this was better. He was free of the army, free of his nagging wife and he had $20,000. Pity about the other $10,000 back in his room but he hadn't had time to stop and get it. It didn't matter. He could still make a new start for himself. All he had to do was reach the border.

Judd and Dell rode through most of the night, stopping only when the sky was at its blackest, and it became dangerous to carry on. Dell, with a soldier's habit of being able to sleep whenever he had the chance, curled up in his blanket and immediately began to snore. But Judd fretted, unable to rest, hoping Woodford wasn't travelling ever further away from them.

The next day it was even hotter, the sun a blazing disc turning the sky a washed-out blue. The going was hard as well, each step the horses took sending sprays of dust round them. When they reached the second creek, it contained barely enough water for the horses to drink and for them to fill their canteens.

To Judd's anger they had spotted no sign of the colonel's trail. Was he wrong? Had the man not done what was expected of him but instead ridden in an entirely different direction away from Mexico? If so they might never catch him.

Now as they rested the horses, Dell crossed to the

far side of the creek. He walked along for a way, studying the ground. Suddenly he turned, signalling to Judd.

'Here, Marshal!'

Judd caught the horses' reins and pulled them away from the water, hurrying to where the sergeant waited.

'Here. This is where he came out of the creek!'

Judd hunkered down. 'And he's not far ahead of us. He must have stopped for at least part of the night as well.'

'He's following the creek before turning off,' Dell said. 'We ought to try to catch up before he reaches the canyonlands. Once among them he'll have a chance to hide his tracks again or find a good spot to set up an ambush.'

'OK. Let's get on. And, Dell, I don't have to tell you, Woodford is a desperate man.'

They were after him! Closing in! Dammit and damn Marshal Judd. But however determined a trouble-maker Judd was, however good a lawman, he too could be surprised. Woodford wasn't going to be taken without a fight. Well, he just wasn't going to be taken at all if he could help it.

Mid-morning, the tracks turned away from the side of the creek to lead up a steep slope littered with rocks and hardy shrub. Judd and Dell came to a halt at the bottom and dismounted. Judd didn't like it. All his instincts were aroused. It was so very quiet.

No bird-song. No sound of small animals skittering out of the way of the horses. And here, indeed, were a number of places where Woodford could hide and fire down at them.

'What's the matter?' Dell asked.

'I'm not sure. It might be nothing. But why don't you go on down the creek a bit further and try to come out on the far side of this slope?'

'You think he's up there?'

'I'm not about to chance he's definitely not.'

'What will you be doing?'

'Climbing the slope.'

Dell looked at Judd. 'You sure?'

'Yeah. If he is there, someone's got to keep him occupied. I'll give you a few minutes to get down the creek a ways.'

'Watch yourself.'

Judd waited five minutes. Then taking several deep breaths he led his horse up the slope, taking the easiest way he could. His scalp prickled. His heart was thudding in his chest. He kept glancing up at the trop of the hill, scared he would see the glint of a rifle barrel, certain he would hear the sound of a shot. He knew the colonel was unlikely to miss. But nothing happened.

He reached the top safely; no one was there. And then his eye caught sight of a spot behind some rocks where the brush was flattened and the earth disturbed. Woodford had, in fact, been lying in ambush. Judd shivered. He'd had a close call.

At the same moment Dell's shout reached his

ears. The sergeant was at the bottom of the slope, waving his hat to attract Judd's attention. He pointed frantically in to the distance.

Woodford! Galloping away!

At once Judd saw what had happened. The colonel had set an ambush but when Judd and Dell split up realized they suspected what he was doing, had thought he wouldn't be able to shoot them both coming at him from two directions. Instead he'd made a run for it.

Stupid bastard! He couldn't get away now.

Heart beating with excitement., Judd vaulted into the saddle and urged his horse into an all-out gallop down to the desert floor. He was soon joined by Dell and the two horses pounded along side by side, raising up a cloud of dust that hung in the air behind them.

They were catching up. Woodford's horse was tiring.

Judd saw Woodford glance over his shoulder. He was now close enough to glimpse his wild eyes. He knew the man would never surrender to him.

As if to prove him right, Woodford fired at them several times. But it was over his shoulder from the back of a speeding horse and the bullets came nowhere near.

Perhaps knowing how useless that was, knowing, too, that he couldn't outrun them, Woodford suddenly dragged his horse to a halt. He half dismounted, half fell out of the saddle, aimed the rifle.

Even as Dell continued the pursuit, Judd was also stopping. He pulled his rifle from its scabbard. The colonel fired once. Twice. He didn't hit his pursuers. Before he could try again Judd returned the fire. Calmly, carefully.

Woodford's arms flailed in the air. Judd watched him take a step forward and then collapse, face down in the desert. He didn't move again.

It was mid-afternoon of the following day when the two men, leading the horse on which the colonel's body was tied, came into sight of the fort.

As they rode towards the parade ground, Judd nudged Dell, 'Look!'

Lieutenant Lucas Mariner sat in the doorway of the post hospital. Thank God he was all right! And there was Angela by his side, holding his hand.

Judd grinned, 'Fancy having a lieutenant for a son-in-law?'

'Umm, coming up in the world,' Dell replied.

Judd laughed. 'I suppose you'll have to call him sir!'